Michael's Spear

Hilton Pashley

THE
DOME
PRESS

For Laura, Leyla and Lillian

'*Everything has to come to an end, sometime.*'
L. Frank Baum, The Marvellous Land of Oz

Contents

Chapter 1

Webs

'So what do you think of my plan, Mr Flay?' asked Lilith, gently smoothing the long skirt of her sheer, red, spider-silk dress.

Flay stared up at her with a preternaturally calm face. There was no emotion in its perfect lines, no love, no hate, no joy, no sadness, just a hint of implacable will crouching behind those vivid, green eyes. Unlike many demons of his clan he chose to appear in his natural form: a long-boned, almost elfin face, framed at the ears and chin with black scales. His skull was shaved, and the skin inked with a series of curling, symmetrical tattoos.

'I think it has... merit,' he replied.

'Just merit?' said Lilith, scowling. 'You're a cold fish, aren't you, Flay? Not at all like your cousins, may they rest in peace.'

'Rook, Raven and Crow of the Corvidae were amateurs,' said Flay. 'Circus clowns in bowler hats, playing at being killers. They tried to kidnap Jonathan and they failed miserably. Their spectacular deaths are an example to those demons who delude themselves into thinking they are assassins, but have neither the temperament nor skill to be successful.'

'By successful I assume you mean not being incinerated, or having your head knocked off with a cricket bat?'

The merest hint of a smile tugged at the corner of Flay's mouth.

'See, you aren't entirely humourless,' Lilith said, rising from her throne.

Flay watched as Lilith, queen of the silk garden and his employer, glided down the cobwebbed steps to stand before him. She was tall and painfully thin, her face covered with a veil of the same silk from which her dress was made. Flay could just make out her jet black eyes glittering behind the translucent material.

'We have to be careful, Flay,' said Lilith. 'I am the last Archdemon, and I don't wish to meet the same unfortunate end as my two colleagues. Belial was clumsy, Baal was insane, but I... I will be as a surgeon. I will study, wait and, when the time is right, I will put my plan into action. I even have my scalpel... See?'

Flay looked at the table next to Lilith where an object was covered with a white silk sheet. He knew what was beneath it, but he indulged his mistress in her show of theatrics as she gently twitched the sheet aside. There, resting in an onyx cradle, lay a spear made from a single piece of black glass. Runes carved into the haft glittered redly, and the blade flickered with a corona of crimson fire.

'It's mine now,' said Lilith. 'It has taken centuries, but finally I have it completely under my control. The Archangel Sammael may have made this for her brother, Michael, but now it will serve as *my* instrument. Sammael's battle with Baal has given me the opening I need finally to make my move.' She stroked the spear lovingly and the runes flared at her touch. 'I will succeed where Belial and Baal failed. All creation will tremble at my footsteps.'

'And what are you going to do about Lucifer?' asked Flay.

Lilith smiled. 'Oh, once he has served his purpose I'll make sure he can't interfere. He's already a fly trapped in my web. They all are, they just don't know it yet. The most dangerous enemy is the one you can't see coming, and they won't know what they're up against until it's far too late to stop me. It's already begun, Flay. One day soon I will be a goddess, and every living thing will be mine to dispose of as I see fit!'

Chapter 2

What's in the Box?

'I wonder what Lucifer's up to?' said Jonathan, sitting at the kitchen table in the Hobbes End vicarage and cramming the last of his breakfast into his mouth. 'Why would he ask everyone in the village to meet on the green at midday?'

'I don't know,' said Savantha from the depths of the pantry. 'Perhaps he's bringing us a Christmas present? What do you think, Elgar?'

The cat popped his head over the rim of the kitchen sink, soap suds adorning his ears. 'I haven't got a clue, you never know with him. Now stop interrupting my morning bath.' The cat sank out of sight and gave a contented sigh.

'What are you doing, little demon?' said Savantha, striding back into the kitchen. 'That's my clean washing-up water!'

'And it's being used for washing,' said the cat, scrubbing behind his ears with a white-socked paw.

Savantha sighed and turned to her son. 'Well, you were

hungry,' she said to Jonathan, 'a full English breakfast demolished in less than three minutes. Impressive.'

He smiled. 'Yeah, I don't want to miss saying goodbye to Ignatius and Grimm. They'll be leaving for Devon in a minute.'

A car horn sounded from outside. 'Looks like they're ready,' said Jonathan. 'Come on, let's see them off.' He got up to get his coat, closely followed by a foam-covered Elgar. 'Wait for me,' said the cat, shaking himself furiously in a vain attempt to dry his fur.

They walked down the drive to the gates, the snow crunching under their feet. It was a crisp, winter day, and the village looked positively magical under its covering of white. Leaning against an old Daimler was Ignatius Crumb, the vicar of Hobbes End, a long winter coat over the top of his usual tweeds.

'Ah, there you are,' said Ignatius. 'We need to get going. It's a long hike to Devon and there's more snow forecast.'

'And Constance will fret if we're late,' said Ignatius' friend Grimm. His massive frame was shoe-horned into the driver's seat, and the battered bowler hat that he'd won in his battle with the demon, Rook, perched on top of his bald head.

'How long are you staying with your mother?' asked Jonathan.

'Just a couple of days,' said Ignatius. 'We'll be back before Christmas Eve as long as we don't get snowed in.'

'Give her my love,' said Savantha. 'It's been ages since I've seen her.'

'I will,' said Ignatius, climbing into the car. 'Right, while we're away Savantha's in charge, not that we're expecting any chaos. Everything's been mercifully quiet of late; let's hope it stays that way.'

'Can Stubbs and I be in charge too?' asked Montgomery from his perch on top of the gatepost. As one of the pair of gargoyles that had guarded the vicarage for over a century he took his role as protector very seriously.

'Like I could stop you,' said Ignatius. On top of the opposite gatepost Stubbs rubbed his granite paws together in glee. 'You know the drill. No flying unless you have to and no snowball fights near any windows.'

'Wouldn't dream of it,' mumbled the gargoyles in unison.

'Can't we have a daily rota for who's in charge?' asked Elgar, jumping onto the bonnet of the car.

'No!' said Grimm. 'If we left you in command, all we'd have when we got back was a large grocery bill for kippers, ice cream and flea powder.'

'Harsh!' said Elgar. 'But probably true. Off you pop then.'

'And on that note we shall away,' said Ignatius. 'Sorry to miss Lucifer's announcement but Devon is calling. I'm sure you'll tell us all about it when we get back.'

The Daimler's engine roared into life and Elgar leapt off

the bonnet. As the car pulled away Grimm stuck his head out of the window. 'And no funny business with my tea collection!'

'Oh, just you wait,' said Elgar with a devilish grin. 'Just you wait.'

'What are you up to for the rest of the day, darling?' Savantha asked Jonathan once they'd returned to the vicarage kitchen.

'Apart from finding out what Lucifer wants, I don't know,' he said. It had been several months since they'd rescued his mother from the castle of the Archdemon Baal, and Jonathan was still getting used to her being there with him. Sometimes he would peek into her room at night to make sure he wasn't dreaming, and that she really was there to stay. When she slept, Savantha relaxed the masking spell that hid her true form, that of a demon princess. Against the white of her pillow, Jonathan could see the red scales that patterned her neck, and the curve of the horns that grew from her forehead. Only the dull ache of his angel father's death marred the depth of the love he felt for his mum.

Jonathan continued to mask his own true appearance out of habit. He was the only half-angel, half-demon in existence, and despite being surrounded by friends and family it could be lonely at times. Even he didn't know what he was capable of, and so he chose to hide the little horns on his forehead, the scales on his neck, and even his magnificent wings. After all that had happened over the last year, he just wanted to fit in and be normal for as long as he could.

He looked across the kitchen table at Savantha's hands cradling a mug of tea. The wounds inflicted by Baal on her palms had healed beautifully, partly due to her demon physiology, but also due to the care and attention that Grimm had paid to her. He'd been an army doctor and fixing things was second nature to him. The big man had seemed almost shy in Savantha's presence, but as her hands healed Grimm suggested she try learning to play the piano to strengthen them. They were often to be found together now, Savantha struggling with a fiddly bit of Mozart as Grimm sat in an armchair and listened to her play with his eyes closed. When Jonathan thought about it he wasn't sure how it made him feel. Grimm was a brave and gentle giant who'd faced an Archdemon armed only with a cricket bat. There was nothing he wouldn't do for his friends; he'd even left the army to come and look after Ignatius when the vicar had lost his wife and son in a car crash. Although Jonathan missed his dad terribly, he thought the world of Grimm and was glad his mum had such kind company. Can you be happy and sad at the same time, he wondered?

'Penny for them?' asked Savantha, smiling at her son over the top of her mug.

'Just... just thinking,' said Jonathan, feeling his cheeks redden.

Savantha nodded, giving him a knowing look. 'So, what do you want for Christmas?'

'I hadn't thought about it,' he said. 'After all that's happened this year, asking for a smartphone seems a bit... well... silly.' He paused. 'I have everything I could want now, everything that matters except...'

'Your dad?' asked Savantha, reaching out and giving her son's hand a squeeze.

Jonathan nodded.

'I miss him too,' said Savantha. 'Come on, let's go and put some fresh flowers on the graves of our loved ones and know they are watching over us.'

Jonathan smiled at his mother. Taking her hand, they walked out of the vicarage and over to the village shop which was run by Mr and Mrs Forrester, the parents of Jonathan's friend Cay. They were half-way across the green when they saw something quite lovely. Outside the shop, a wolf with red fur was sitting on her haunches in front of Mr Peters, one of the many inhabitants of Hobbes End. The old man, dressed in his usual black coat, hat and sunglasses, was tenderly stroking the fur on the wolf's head.

'Cay's really enjoying being a werewolf, isn't she?' said Savantha.

Jonathan nodded. 'I don't know what I'd have done

without her when I first arrived here,' he said. 'I felt so alone and she helped me fit in. I'm very lucky to know her.'

'That you are,' said Savantha. 'She's incredibly strong for one so young. Without her we wouldn't have defeated Baal.'

'Yeah,' said Jonathan, remembering. Cay had saved the day despite being badly injured on her solo journey into Hell – a stunt that her father had described as both *stupid* and *magnificent*. 'You wouldn't think that Cay used to torment Mr Peters,' said Jonathan. 'Now they're the best of mates.'

'Why would she torment Mr Peters?' asked Savantha.

'She thought he was a vampire, and kept trying to prove it by seeing if ultraviolet light would make him burst into flames.'

'The little monkey!' Savantha laughed.

Mr Peters got slowly to his feet, and waved to Cay as she sped off into the forest. '*Auf Wiedersehen!*' he called out, a big smile on his wrinkled face. He spotted Jonathan and his mother and walked over to them.

'She is brave, that little one,' he said.

'Yeah, she is,' agreed Jonathan.

'It's a fine day for a run,' said Mr Peters. 'She's going to see if she can find Brass. Ignatius asked our resident mechanical dragon to locate a suitable Christmas tree for the village green.'

'I don't think Brass will be hard to find,' said Jonathan,

nodding at the tracks from the village pond where the dragon spent most of her time asleep beneath the water.

'Ach, let *meine kleine rote Wolfin* have her sport,' said Mr Peters. 'Where are you both off to on such a beautiful morning?'

'Just buying some flowers and then going to the churchyard,' said Savantha.

'Ah,' Mr Peters nodded his understanding. 'Then may I accompany you? It is good to remember those we have loved.'

Just for a moment Jonathan saw the strangest look flicker across the old man's face, but it was gone before he could figure out what it might mean.

'Shall we?' asked Mr Peters, extending an arm to Savantha.

She smiled and took it, and together they walked into the shop.

It was shortly before midday when a grating noise disturbed the peace of the village. 'What's that?' asked Montgomery.

'It's probably Brass coming back with a Christmas tree,' mumbled Stubbs, as he gingerly brushed snow from his ears.

'You still worried about them falling off again?' said Montgomery.

'My ears didn't *fall* off!' growled Stubbs. 'One got knocked off when a block of stone the size of Grimm's

Daimler fell on me, and the other was knocked off when I got slammed against the church wall and through the lychgate during our battle with Baal. There was no *falling off* of any body parts.'

'Sorry I mentioned it,' said Montgomery. 'At least Jonathan knows how to fix them.'

'Yeah, there is that,' agreed Stubbs. 'I can't see Brass, by the way, and that noise is getting louder. Time for a look I think.'

They hopped off their perches and walked to the green. 'It's coming from the portal to Heaven,' said Montgomery. 'I hope it's nothing nasty. I've had a gutful of nasty for this year.'

'You and me both,' agreed Stubbs.

In front of them, a hole in reality stood on the snow-covered grass. As wide and high as a pair of cathedral doors, the portal had been opened by the Archangel Sammael, Jonathan's great-aunt, in order to gain access to the gates of Heaven in the search for Jonathan's father. At first the portal had been a source of wonder, but now, as with all the unusual things that happened in Hobbes End, it had been accepted as completely normal.

The gargoyles arrived just in time to see a massive, humanoid creature emerge, dragging a large wooden crate behind it. Once it had got the crate onto the village green, it stood aside and waited, completely motionless.

'Umm?' said Montgomery.

'Sorry for the intrusion,' said a voice.

The gargoyles looked round. Lucifer was dressed in grubby work clothes and looked tired, but there was a hint of a grin at the corner of his mouth.

'Do you like my construct? It's not in your league of course – I don't have Gabriel's skills in that regard – but it is handy. I made it from the weapons that the demon army dropped when we fought Baal.'

'Ooer!' said Montgomery, walking over to the construct and tapping its leg. There was a hollow, metallic sound, like an out-of-tune bell. The construct looked down at the little gargoyle and harrumphed.

'What's it called?' asked Stubbs.

Lucifer looked momentarily perplexed. 'I have absolutely no idea,' he said. 'I hadn't really thought of giving it a name.'

'It must have a name,' said Montgomery. 'How about Albert? That's a good name.'

'Or Susan,' said Stubbs.

'I'm not sure it looks much like a Susan,' said Lucifer, trying very hard not to smile.

'I dub thee Albert!' said Montgomery in triumph, giving the construct another whack on the leg. The newly christened Albert rolled his eyes in response.

'What's in the box?' asked Stubbs, annoyed that his choice of name had been dismissed out of hand.

'It's a surprise,' said Lucifer.

'Hi!' said Jonathan, as he arrived with Elgar and Savantha. 'Well, this is all very mysterious. How are you? I haven't seen you in ages.'

'Thank you, Jonathan,' said Lucifer, shaking his hand in greeting. 'I'm well and I've been rather... busy.'

Jonathan looked at the fallen angel. There was something odd in the way Lucifer was acting. It felt very out of character and made Jonathan wonder just what the ruler of Hell had been up to.

'This is Albert,' said Montgomery, clambering up the construct to sit happily upon its head. Albert didn't seem to mind this familiarity and idly scratched his nose with a forefinger the size of a large sausage. The screeching noise made Jonathan wince.

'It looks more like a Susan to me,' said Elgar.

'See,' said Stubbs.

'Enough!' said Lucifer. '*Albert* is not the sharpest chisel but he's very helpful for fetching and carrying, which is what I need most right now. I've brought something to show you which I think you might be interested in.'

'Ooh,' said Jonathan, wondering what was in the crate.

'No spoilers though,' said Lucifer. 'I want everyone here to see this.'

'Ignatius and Grimm send their apologies,' said Savantha. 'They've gone to Devon but will be back in a couple of days.'

Lucifer nodded. 'Then they'll have a nice surprise upon their return.' He stood and waited while the inhabitants of Hobbes End, curious as to why they had been asked to gather on the green, came out of their homes and stood round the portal.

'Where's Cay?' asked Lucifer. 'I would have thought she'd be first in the queue to see what I've brought.'

'She's off running in the forest,' said Jonathan. 'I'm sure she'll be back soon though.'

'Tcch, werewolves,' said Lucifer, rolling his eyes in mock irritation.

'Ahem,' said Cay's father, raising his eyebrows at Lucifer. Cay had inherited her abilities from her dad and he was a bit sensitive about the subject.

'No offence intended, Kenneth,' said Lucifer, nodding respectfully to Mr Forrester where he stood with his arm around his wife.

'Here comes Sam,' said Jonathan, nodding in the direction of his great-aunt's windmill. With the hem of her long black coat brushing against the surface of the snow, Sammael Morningstar, the last Archangel, looked as though she was floating across the green. Her dark coat and gloves were in stark contrast to her pale skin, and with her white, unbound hair spread across her shoulders, Jonathan thought his great-aunt looked like some strange spirit of winter.

'Hello, old friend,' she said, taking Lucifer's hands in greeting. 'To what do we owe the honour of this visit?'

'Well now,' replied Lucifer. 'I have a surprise for you and Jonathan and I wanted everyone to see it.'

Sammael nodded. 'OK. So, what's in the box?'

Lucifer smiled to himself and turned to his construct. 'Albert, remove the lid, if you would be so kind.'

With a metallic creak, Albert reached over to the box with his massive hands. Jonathan held his breath in excitement. For once he knew that this was going to be a nice surprise. Albert had just grasped the top of the crate when a searing pain ripped through Jonathan's abdomen. He sank to his knees with a gasp; it was as if someone was cutting him open. Through waves of agony he was dimly aware of Sammael collapsing to the frozen ground, her thrashing limbs carving out a twisted snow-angel on the green.

'What is this?' roared Lucifer, huge, bat-like wings springing up and out from his back. Jonathan reached out a hand and the fallen angel grasped it.

'What's wrong?' Lucifer demanded. 'Tell me.'

Jonathan was in so much pain he could barely form words. In the months since his arrival his bond to Hobbes End had grown deep. When his grandfather, the Archangel Gabriel, had crash-landed in the village pond all those centuries ago, he'd given away the power held in his wings to gift Hobbes End the equivalent of a soul. In return, the village did its best to protect those who came to live in it. Now it was screaming in Jonathan's head; it was being hurt, and hurt badly. Abruptly the pain ceased, but the sense of Hobbes End being terribly wounded remained.

'The village is under attack,' he gasped.

'By who?' asked Stubbs. 'I can't see anything.'

'There's something happening,' shouted Montgomery, from his viewpoint on top of Albert's head. I can see trees thrashing about right at the edge of the forest!'

To hammer the point home, a mighty roar erupted from deep within the trees, closely followed by the howl of a wolf.

'That's Brass,' said Elgar.

'And Cay,' said Jonathan. 'Something awful is happening. We need to get to them. Now!'

Chapter 3

A Bit Loose at the Seams

Brass carefully picked her way through the forest as she hunted for a Christmas tree. She'd seen just the one she needed a few weeks previously and was determined to return with her prize. Frost rimed her magnificent scales and, perched on the end of a long, serpentine neck, her head bobbed this way and that as she peered through the undergrowth.

She was Gabriel's masterpiece, and after being alone for so many years Brass was very happy to be living in Hobbes End. Even though Gabriel had sacrificed himself to destroy the Archdemon Belial, Brass found that sleeping at the bottom of the village pond – close to where her creator had landed – was comforting.

Her eyes grew wide as she sensed something change in the air, something very, very wrong. Static danced across her vast, metallic bulk and she sniffed loudly, trying to locate the source of the disturbance. It didn't take her long to find it – barely a hundred meters away, close to where the trees gave way to open fields.

With a low growl building in her belly, Brass gave up on delicacy and launched herself forward, crashing through the forest like a Challenger tank. Knocking over trees and flattening bushes, she burst into a clearing and came skidding to a halt. In front of her, a jagged rip in reality shuddered and flexed, gnawing at the weave of creation like a ravening beast. Air was sucked through the gap and into the void beyond with incredible force, and Brass had to ram her foreclaws into the frozen ground to stop herself being swallowed into oblivion. Raising her head she bellowed at the sky, doing her best to alert the village that something terrible was happening.

As the echoes of her cry faded she sensed something else. Brass may just have been a construct, but whatever this was it made her heaven-forged scales crawl. She'd never felt anything like it. Nothing in the sentience that Gabriel had given her prepared the dragon for the wave of cold, implacable, ancient malice that poured through the rip. It made her want to turn and flee, but instead she dug her claws in deeper and roared in defiance.

Slowly, as if uncertain of what they might find, the tips of four, black, oily-looking tentacles poked through the wound. On the underside of each limb, suckers ringed with jagged teeth dripped a virulent, green ichor onto the snow. It smoked where it fell, an alien poison that ate its way into the earth like acid.

Brass shuddered as she felt the village cry out in pain.

Desperate to protect her home, she shot her head forward and snapped at the tentacles as they writhed in the air. Quick though she was, they whipped back with even greater speed, one of them smacking her across the face with impossible force. The impact dented her scales and left a trail of corrosion across the metal. Brass realised she was in serious trouble.

A wolf howled and Cay appeared at the edge of the clearing, her teeth bared and her fur standing on end. Before Cay could react, the awful pull of the rushing air caught her. Scrambling frantically in the snow, she tumbled head over heels towards the rip and the creature that lay within it.

In an explosion of snow, dead leaves and branches, Brass reached out with her right wing and snatched Cay as she shot past, saving her from a horrible fate. With a grunt of effort the dragon swept her wing backwards, pinning Cay safely against her side. It wasn't gentle, but it was necessary. Cay howled again, this time in terror as she huddled against the reassuring bulk of Brass' body.

More tentacles emerged from the void. They gripped the edges of the rip and pulled, straining to widen it. Behind them, a vast, cyclopean eye with a pupil of deepest black peered at the dragon and the wolf, swivelling this way and that as it studied its prey. Surging forward, it squeezed its loathsome body through the gap and into Hobbes End.

Brass reared up, ready to unleash her greatest weapon. She'd never had occasion to use it before, but Gabriel had thought of everything when he'd designed her. Taking a deep breath, Brass opened her jaws and blasted the creature with a torrent of white fire. It gave an unearthly shriek as flames tore into it, shrivelling the alien flesh and driving it back.

The dragon grinned but her triumph was cut short. The creature withdrew its damaged tentacles, only to grow fresh ones from its pulsating body. Enraged beyond measure it flung itself at the rip once more, battering Brass from all directions. Unwilling to run, the dragon bit and tore at her foe, her scales buckling under the onslaught. She tried to launch another blast of fire but the creature wrapped a tentacle around her massive jaws and squeezed. Hampered by the need to protect Cay, Brass couldn't leap out of range. All she could do was hold her position and hope that help would arrive, preferably before she was reduced to a smoking heap of twisted metal.

In answer to her prayers, a flash of black plummeted from above. The creature squealed as three of its limbs flopped twitching to the ground, severed with surgical precision as Sammael Morningstar landed in front of the dragon. From her shoulders sprang the mighty wings of an Archangel, a lethal and glorious fan of midnight-hued ribbons, each filled with a never-ending stream of mathematics too complex to comprehend. Sammael let Jonathan go from where she'd been holding him to her chest as she flew, and he too manifested his wings: ribbons of imperial purple with serrated edges. Standing side by side with Sammael he joined her in attacking the creature that threatened their home and friends.

Lucifer hovered above them, his vast, bat-like wings spread wide. A sphere of white light leapt from his outstretched hands and flew across the clearing, striking the massive eye and blossoming into a huge fireball. Bathed in hellfire, a hideous scream burst from the creature as it recoiled in pain.

No longer blocked by the alien's grotesque body, air rushed back into the rip once again. Jonathan and Sammael held on to Brass' forelegs as Lucifer dropped to sit astride the dragon's back, his face thunderous.

'What the hell is that?' asked Jonathan, over the shrieking wind.

'Consequences!' Lucifer shouted, looking pointedly at Sammael. 'I warned you this might happen. You couldn't just settle for killing Baal, could you? I know he destroyed Heaven; I know he left Jonathan's father to die of his wounds; but this is what happens when you go too far. You used your wings to rip open reality, just so you could fling Baal's rotten soul out of creation and into eternal torment. You've damaged the weave of creation, and there are things outside this universe of ours that want in. They can sense weak points and that...' he said, pointing at the creature that writhed in smoking agony, 'is just a baby.'

Jonathan gulped. Just a baby? It was the size of a house.

'We need to repair the damage,' shouted Sammael. 'I need your help, Jonathan. Take my hand.'

Jonathan did as she asked, the rushing wind making his eyes water. He watched the huge creature as it flailed its tentacles, silently wishing he was somewhere else. That *thing* was so alien, so filled with malice, that it filled him with an awful mix of fear and revulsion. 'What do you want me to do?' he asked.

'Let me see Gabriel's memories,' she said. 'I need his finesse for this. I don't want this repair to be temporary.'

Jonathan nodded, closed his eyes, and felt the presence of his great-aunt inside his head. Once again he was standing at a table in the virtual library Gabriel had bequeathed to him, only this time he was not alone: Sammael was beside him.

'This is astonishing!' she said. 'What a gift my brother has given you.'

'Yeah,' said Jonathan. 'It is. All his knowledge in one place.'

'How do I...?'

'You just think about the information you need. When I first came here I had to go and find the right book, but now it comes to me and pops itself on this table.'

'Then ask for something on quantum stitching,' said Sammael.

'Quantum stitching?' asked Jonathan. 'What on earth is that?'

'Trust me,' said Sammael. 'Think of it as embroidery for angels.'

Jonathan concentrated, asking the library for something that would help them repair the rip. In the blink of an eye a book appeared on the table before them, it was titled, *Cosmic Knitting for Dummies*.

'Hah!' said Sammael. 'I love you, too, brother.'

She opened the book, placed her hand on the pages and immediately knew what had to be done. 'Let's go,' she said.

Faster than thought, they were back in the clearing, hanging on to Brass and staring into the void. Reaching out with her wing ribbons, Sammael carefully inserted them into the edges of the rip.

'You really need to hurry,' said Jonathan.

'I'm going as fast as I can,' said Sammael. 'This is tricky.'

'That thing is coming back and it looks really annoyed.'

'I'm very aware of the extra-dimensional squid that wants to gatecrash,' she said, her eyes screwed shut in concentration. 'If I do this wrong I could tear the whole world open. Just... shush!'

Jonathan clamped his mouth shut and gripped Sammael's hand tightly. As he watched, the edges of the rip began to glow with white light and oh-so-slowly they knitted together. Beyond the shrinking gap, the creature gave a bellow and launched itself at them. Jonathan could only stare in horror as the huge eye grew larger and larger.

'SAM!' he shouted.

'Done!' said Sammael triumphantly, sweat pouring down her face. With a loud zipping noise the edges of the rip slammed shut, just as two tentacles darted through. With an awful squelch the alien appendages plopped to the floor, their poison staining the snowy ground a diseased black. The wind dropped, leaves fluttered to the ground, and all was suddenly quiet.

Jonathan let out a shuddering sigh as Sammael looked at him, her face weary but relieved. A black shape jumped onto Brass' foreleg and peered at Jonathan.

'Well, that was all a bit tense,' said Elgar. 'If it wasn't for Stubbs sitting on my tail, I'd have been sucked through that gap and ended my days as a cat-canapé for tentacle boy.' He shuddered.

Lucifer strode forward and peered at where the rip had been. 'I think you did it,' he said to Sammael without turning round. Jonathan had to agree. His great-aunt had indeed stitched reality back together with extraordinary skill, although something about the rip bothered Jonathan. He didn't know why, but thinking about it with the benefit of Gabriel's memories and knowledge made him uneasy.

He rubbed his forehead and exhaled, putting his jitters down to the fact the universe had almost unravelled in front of his eyes.

Sammael walked over to stand next to Lucifer. 'Consequences,' she said sadly.

Lucifer nodded and raised an eyebrow. 'I'm not one to say I told you so but... I told you so.'

Jonathan saw Sammael's cheeks redden. Opening gates *within* this reality was tricky at best; it had to be done with great care to avoid weakening the threads that held the weave of creation together. Lost inside her rage when she killed the Archdemon Baal, Sammael had ignored the risks and caused incredible damage. That act was now coming back to haunt her, just as Lucifer had said it would.

'Why here?' said Jonathan, hoping Sammael wasn't feeling too guilty.

'Hmm?' she said.

'Why did the rip open here? Why not somewhere near Baal's castle in Hell where we fought him?'

'Good question,' said Lucifer. 'It may be because of the battering this village has had recently – the attack by Belial and then Baal – plus the gate to Heaven has been open for months.'

'Maybe,' said Jonathan, but he wasn't entirely convinced. There was something nagging at the back of his mind but he couldn't figure out what it was. More and more he saw things with his grandfather's eyes, and somehow this didn't fit.

Brass snorted in anger as she examined the damage to her scales.

'We'll fix that,' said Jonathan, and the dragon grinned at him, showing her full array of wickedly sharp teeth.

Cay trotted out from behind Brass' wing, closely followed by the gargoyles. She sat on her haunches next to Jonathan and whined. 'You OK?' he asked her.

She nodded, but her yellow eyes were still wide with fright.

'Well, there's nothing more to be done right now,' said Lucifer. 'Let's hope no more of these things appear when we're not around to fix them.'

'Yeah,' said Jonathan, wondering what carnage would be caused if a rip suddenly appeared at school, or in the middle of London in rush hour.

'I'm still waiting to find out what's in that box,' said Montgomery.

'Oh yes,' said Lucifer. 'I'd quite forgotten that in all the excitement. Let's walk back to the village and I'll show you.'

Jonathan stayed where he was for a moment with Elgar and Cay sitting by his side.

'What's up?' asked the cat. 'Are you going to say something portentous like, *there's a storm coming?*'

'I don't know,' said Jonathan. He didn't want to believe

it, but he had an awful feeling that the peace of the last six months was about to be shattered in a quite spectacular manner.

Chapter 4

Home Improvements

Jonathan arrived back in Hobbes End to find the whole village still gathered on the green. Mr Forrester walked over, his face grave.

'I gather there was a bit of trouble,' he said, looking meaningfully at his daughter. Cay – still in her wolf form – studiously avoided his gaze.

'Yeah,' said Jonathan. 'Another apocalypse averted just in the nick of time.'

'Well, you can't say life here is ever dull,' said Mr Forrester. 'While you were off saving the world, the vicarage phone was ringing off the hook so I took the liberty of answering it. Ignatius was chewing his arm off with worry. Even in the car he could tell something was up.'

'Oh no!' said Jonathan, remembering the vicar was as closely bonded to Hobbes End as he and Sammael were. 'He's not going to come back, is he? He doesn't see his mum very often.'

'He's fine now,' said Mr Forrester. 'I reassured him that

everything was OK. Sammael called him back and I assume she's filled him in on what happened.'

'Phew,' said Jonathan. Ignatius took his duties so seriously and had been through so much. Jonathan hated the idea that his friend couldn't even have a few days away without fretting about what might be going wrong in his absence.

'Right, you,' Mr Forrester said to Cay. 'You'd better come indoors and get changed, out of that fur and into some warm clothes.'

Cay whined and flattened her ears.

'Oh stop sulking,' said Mr Forrester. 'If you hurry up you can see what's in the mysterious crate that... um... big metal chap is guarding.'

'His name's Albert,' said Elgar.

'Is it indeed?' said Mr Forrester. 'He doesn't look like an Albert.'

'Oh let's not do this again,' said the cat. 'Come on, Jonny, let's go and watch the grand opening of said box.'

Cay shot inside the village shop, desperate not to miss out on the big surprise. Lucifer had taken up his place again next to Albert and looked quietly pleased with himself.

A minute later Cay joined them, still pulling on her jumper.

'It's inside out,' said Elgar.

'I don't care!' she said, hurrying to tie her mass of auburn hair into a ponytail. 'I want to see this.'

Jonathan saw Sammael walking back from the direction of the vicarage, and he prayed that the Daimler wouldn't be screeching to a halt beside them anytime soon. She saw his quizzical look and gave him a brief thumbs-up.

'Good,' said Jonathan, pleased that Ignatius and Grimm's trip hadn't been ruined.

'So, why all the theatrics?' asked Elgar, pointing at the crate.

'Pfft!' snorted Lucifer. 'You need to appreciate the finer points of showmanship. Watch and learn.'

He beckoned Jonathan and Sammael to him and Jonathan watched the fallen angel's face closely as he walked over. Lucifer shone with his usual pride in feeling generally superior to everyone – and everything – else in creation, but there was something behind those piercing eyes. Jonathan couldn't quite believe it but he looked... nervous. What could Lucifer have possibly done that would make him worry about what anyone else thought? It just wasn't in his nature.

'So then,' said a smiling Sammael. 'What's in the box?'

Lucifer grinned back and nodded to his construct. 'Albert, if you please?'

With a creak and rattle, Albert slowly reached out his massive hands and pried the lid off the crate. An ethereal light burst outward, and everyone craned forward to have a look at what lay within. When Jonathan saw what nestled upon a bed of fine wood-shavings, a lump formed in his throat and he turned to Lucifer. He tried to say something but he couldn't find the words.

'Well?' asked Lucifer. 'What do you think?'

Jonathan looked at the contents of the crate once again. Of all the things he'd expected to see, this wasn't one of them. Lucifer had pulled a rabbit out of the hat once again, and the results meant more to Jonathan than anyone could possibly imagine. What he had shattered to free the souls of a multitude of trapped angels, Lucifer had made whole. The fallen angel had done the seemingly impossible: he'd re-forged the gates of Heaven.

'Oh my,' gasped Sammael, as hushed whispers of excitement rippled through the crowd.

'How...?' croaked Jonathan, unable to finish the sentence.

'Well, it took quite a bit of work and I had to swear the angels on guard to secrecy, but I thought you might appreciate the gesture. I did want it to be a surprise.'

Jonathan finally understood the unusual look on Lucifer's face. This was his way of trying to make up for the things he had done. It was his way of saying sorry.

'You magnificent man,' said Sammael, leaning over to kiss Lucifer on the cheek.

To the astonishment of all, he blushed. Lucifer actually blushed. 'Ah, it was nothing,' he said, fluttering his hands about in discomfiture and trying to hide the fact that he was rather pleased with the reaction to his gift.

Elgar jumped onto Jonathan's shoulder to get a better look. 'Wow!' said the cat. 'That is something.'

Jonathan nodded. He'd destroyed the gates of Heaven in a moment of dire need, even though it had broken his heart to do so, and now here they were, whole and in miniature. Lying there at the bottom of the crate were two sheets of impossibly delicate glass, three metres long and one metre across. They were edged in gold leaf, and within them ran the quantum equations of creation, a constant flow of scarlet symbols that boggled the mind with both their complexity and their beauty.

'They seem a bit small,' said Elgar. 'Just saying.'

'Ah, the idiocy of youth,' said Lucifer. 'I neither have the time, the desire, or the patience to explain the procedure in a way that your tiny feline bonce could absorb. Just trust that they will fit perfectly.'

'All right, all right. No need to get all hoity-toity!'

Lucifer scratched the cat affectionately behind the ears.

'They're not finished yet, are they?' said Jonathan, letting the aura of the gates wash over him. He could see them with his grandfather's eyes, feel them with Gabriel's heart, know them like an engineer.

'Oh, you are good,' said Lucifer. 'The old boy would be so proud of you. No, they're not ready yet, that's another reason I brought them here. I want you and Sammael to finish them together.'

'How?' asked Jonathan.

'Colours,' said Sammael. 'They need the colours of our wings to make them complete: a rainbow of mathematics.'

Jonathan finally understood and he smiled. The symbols that flowed through the glass were not enough, they waited for others to join them, make them whole at last. He didn't even have to think about it, he manifested his wings and gently laid the imperial purple ribbons on the gates. Through them he could feel himself adrift on a sea of numbers. Not really understanding how, he felt the glass take something from his wings, something that made him who and what he was. He sensed Sammael doing the same and, as he watched, two new streams of symbols flowed through the glass, one coloured purple, and the other black. The mathematics of creation were complete once more, and the gates... lived.

Jonathan and Sammael drew back from the crate and stood for a moment, looking at what they had helped re-create.

'They're even more beautiful than I remember them,' said Savantha, appearing at her son's side and putting an arm round him.

'We're not finished yet,' said Lucifer. 'Albert, if you would be so kind?'

The construct grabbed hold of the ropes once more, carefully pulling the crate towards the plaza outside Heaven. Everyone followed as Albert made his slow way through the portal, across the marble, and finally came to a halt outside the walls of Heaven itself. Jonathan stared at the gap where the gates used to hang, it was like a missing front tooth and it felt wrong, deficient.

With delicacy that belied his size, Albert lifted the gates from the crate and carefully placed them in the gap. Astonishingly they stayed upright, two sheets of beautiful, shining crystal.

'What do we do now?' Jonathan asked Lucifer.

'*We* don't need to do anything,' the fallen angel replied. 'Heaven knows...'

Jonathan was about to say that he had no idea what Lucifer was talking about when the gates began to grow. Slowly at first, but then with increasing speed the glass stretched out and upward, bonding with the stone and meeting in the middle. Higher and higher the gates grew, until they were just as Jonathan had first encountered them on the quest to find his father, their tops so far above they couldn't be seen with the naked eye. There was a moment of hush, and then a single musical note rang out across the plaza. It was a simple sound, but it contained such joy that everyone present felt it resonate inside their hearts.

'Now it's finished,' said Lucifer. 'Job's a good 'un, as they say.' He smiled at Jonathan. 'What do you think? Are they a suitable replacement?'

Jonathan nodded and smiled back, but there was something else in Lucifer's words, another meaning that wasn't clear yet.

'Well, I'd better be getting home, I suppose. Come along... Albert.'

'Don't you want to open them and go inside?' Jonathan asked.

Lucifer paused and looked over his shoulder, his face sad. 'Not yet. One day. When I deserve it.' Without elaborating further he walked off to the tunnel that led back to Hell.

'I don't understand,' said Jonathan as Sammael came to stand next to him.

'I think I do,' she said. 'He just needs to forgive himself first. Then he'll be ready.'

Adults! They were so weird sometimes. Jonathan took his great-aunt's hand, and together they walked back to Hobbes End with the rest of the villagers. Behind them, the gates to Heaven opened a fraction, revelling in being entire once more. Inside the glass flowed the scarlet symbols of a man who - if he would only admit it to himself - wanted nothing more than to walk through those gates, and be an angel again.

Chapter 5

A Mighty Heart

'Well that was fun,' said Cay, sitting next to Jonathan in the vicarage kitchen.

'Yeah,' he said. 'I wondered why Lucifer had been so quiet lately.' He took a sip of the hot chocolate Savantha had made for them. 'I'm glad you're getting on well with Mr Peters now. It makes a nice change.'

Cay grinned. 'He calls me his little red wolf.'

'*Meine kleine rote wolfin,*' said Jonathan, mimicking Mr Peters' German accent.

'I think it's rather sweet,' said Cay.

'Yeah, it is,' said Jonathan. He went quiet and furrowed his brow.

'What's up?' asked Cay.

'It's that rip in creation we closed earlier. Something about it doesn't feel right.'

'Giant squid monsters trying to invade our world rarely do,' said Cay.

'True,' said Jonathan. 'The alien was bad enough but there's something bothering me about the rip itself. It feels wrong somehow, unnatural.'

'Is there anything in Gabriel's memories about it?' asked Cay.

'Not that I can find,' said Jonathan. 'It's never happened before.'

'You'll figure it out eventually,' said Cay. 'You always do.'

'Ah, I'm probably worrying about nothing,' said Jonathan, taking another sip of hot chocolate.

The cat flap in the back door banged open as Elgar poked his head inside. He had snowflakes on his whiskers and a look in his eye that spoke of the need for mischief.

'It's still light out,' he said. 'Monty, Stubbs and I were just pondering the wisdom of a snowball fight. Care to partake?'

'I'm in,' said Cay, jumping up from the table.

'Me too,' said Jonathan, grateful for the distraction. 'Prepare for snow-based carnage.'

Grabbing their coats they rushed outside, only to be ambushed by the gargoyles who'd prepared their ammunition in advance. Jonathan and Cay blinked snow from their eyes as Elgar laughed his head off.

'Losers!' he shouted, pelting away with the gargoyles in tow.

'Right then,' said Jonathan, grabbing a handful of snow

and scrunching it in his hands. With Cay at his side, he chased after his friends and began a running battle across the village green. Determined to land a solid hit on the cheeky cat, Jonathan prepared a particularly fine snowball, took careful aim and let fly. The icy-white missile soared through the air and caught Elgar smack on the nose. Knocked off balance, the cat tumbled head over heels and snow-ploughed to a halt.

'Gotcha!' said Jonathan, throwing his hands into the air in triumph.

'A palpable hit,' agreed the gargoyles in unison.

Jonathan was about to take aim at Cay when somebody else's consciousness rammed itself into his skull. He collapsed to the green, dimly aware of cries of alarm as Hobbes End slipped away. He fell through darkness, his body rigid and unresponsive but his mind fully aware. From out of the void some-thing, some-one, called out to him. There were no words, just a vast flood of emotion: pain, fear, anger, and underneath it all a fragile hope. Jonathan wanted to comfort this person, reassure them, but he had no idea how.

'Please...' he cried out in desperation. 'Please stop. You don't need to be so afraid!'

Without warning the onrush ceased, leaving behind it a cavernous silence. The sensation of falling ended and Jonathan hung motionless, blind and helpless in a sea of nothing. Then, from somewhere far away, he heard a huge sigh; it was as if someone had been holding their breath for an eternity, and had finally decided to exhale. There was another moment of silence, and then a sound reverberated out of the vast emptiness that surrounded him: two deep, bass notes close together, as loud as rolling thunder. There was no anger in the sound, just a determination to live.

'Who are you?' Jonathan asked.

There was no reply, but another pair of rumbles buffeted his ears: *thump thump*. They sounded just like a heartbeat.

Jonathan let out a gasp. Something his great-aunt Sammael had said to him months earlier popped into his head; something about her late brother, Michael. *He had a mighty heart that boy*, she'd told him.

'It can't be... You're dead,' Jonathan whispered.

He was answered by yet another *thump thump*, and before he could do or say anything else the darkness disappeared and he felt himself back on the village green. He opened his eyes to see his friends peering down at him through falling snow.

'Are you OK?' asked Stubbs.

'I think so,' said Jonathan, smiling at the way snow had piled up on the gargoyle's head. It made him look like a grumpy Christmas elf.

'What's wrong?' asked Cay, dropping to her knees at Jonathan's side.

'I'm not sure,' he replied. 'For a moment I was somewhere else and someone was calling to me.'

'You haven't eaten one of my special kippers, have you?' asked Elgar as he clambered onto Jonathan's legs and began to wash his whiskers. 'You know, the extra smoky ones with added tabasco sauce. They can give you a funny turn if you're not expecting it.'

'No, it's not that,' said Jonathan, propping himself on his elbows. 'I need to speak to Sam right now. I'm not sure, but I think her brother Michael may still be alive!'

'But that's impossible,' gasped Cay.

'Sam killed him by accident when she was creating a new star,' added Elgar. 'It's difficult to recover from being vaporised!'

'And yet someone just called out to me,' said Jonathan. 'Someone who's lost in the dark and whose will is so strong they refuse to die. Someone with a mighty heart.'

'Could it be possible?' asked Montgomery. 'Could Michael have survived the blast somehow? It's been almost four hundred years since he, uh... died?'

'I dunno,' said Jonathan, clambering to his feet, 'but I need to tell Sam.'

'I think she already knows,' said Cay, nodding in the direction of the Archangel's windmill. Jonathan followed her gaze and saw his great-aunt running towards them across the green. Sammael slid to a halt and grabbed Jonathan's arms, the look on her face one of shock. She kept so still he could see snowflakes settle and melt on her eyelashes. 'Tell me I'm not going mad,' she said, the expression on her face one of yearning. 'Tell me you felt that too.'

'He felt it all right,' said Stubbs. 'Laid him out on the green like he'd been poleaxed.'

'I think Michael might still be alive,' said Jonathan. 'I can hear his heartbeat. I think he wants us to find him.'

Sammael nodded. 'And where do we look?' she asked.

Jonathan was about to say he didn't know when a sound rumbled across the frozen ground towards them: two resonant beats close together, just like a heart. It came from the portal that sat on the green.

Jonathan and Sammael looked at each other in astonishment. Behind them, Cay, Elgar and the gargoyles exchanged confused glances. They couldn't hear anything.

'Is that sound, that... heartbeat, coming from Heaven?' Jonathan asked.

'Yes,' said Sammael. 'But if – miraculously – it *is* Michael, then I don't understand how that can be. We were so far away when the accident happened. How could he end up back here and still be alive somewhere in the wreckage of Heaven?'

'I have no idea,' said Jonathan, giving her a fierce grin. 'Shall we go and find out?'

Sammael placed a hand to her chest. 'Is it wrong for me to pray that my little brother is still alive after all this time?'

'No,' said Jonathan. 'Of course it isn't.' His aunt had spent centuries blaming herself for Michael's death, only to have found out that it wasn't her fault after all. Disguised as a child angel, the Archdemon Baal had infiltrated Heaven and slowly driven Sammael's eldest brother – the Archangel Raphael – insane. In his madness, Raphael had sent Michael, the youngest of the four Archangel siblings, on a false rescue mission to save Sammael just as she was creating a new star. Sure that she had killed Michael she had accepted exile as punishment, leaving Baal to trick Raphael into destroying Heaven and all the angels within it.

Appalled at what he had done, Raphael took his own life and, when Sammael finally discovered the full extent of the Archdemon's crimes, her wrath had been terrible. Baal's destruction at her hands had threatened the very fabric of creation, and Jonathan understood why Lucifer was so angry with her. Knowing the truth behind Michael's apparent death had done much to ease Sammael's pain, but Jonathan could only guess at how the thought of finding her brother *alive* might make his great-aunt feel.

'Well,' he said. 'Shall we go and see just whose mighty heart is calling to us?'

Sammael nodded, and gripping Jonathan's hand she strode with him through the snow towards Heaven, a single, delicate thread of hope pulling them onward.

Chapter 6

I've Missed You

Jonathan came to a stop at the edge of the portal. Through it, he could see the white marble plaza stretching away in all directions. Beyond it, a wide flight of steps led up to Heaven's glorious new gates.

'Perhaps that sound came from Hell?' said Sammael, looking to her left where the hidden tunnel to Lucifer's realm was guarded by a squad of well-armed Seraphim. They saw Sammael looking at them and the commander saluted her, his glossy black armour emblazoned with a single white star.

Thump thump. Again the sound of the unearthly heartbeat rolled towards them. 'No, it's definitely coming from inside Heaven,' said Jonathan.

'That it is,' Sammael agreed. 'The question is where?' She turned to Cay who was standing at her side, Elgar and the gargoyles at her feet. 'I know you want to come with us, Cay, but this is not the time. You know your parents are still wary of allowing you out after your *stupid-magnificent* stunt.'

Cay nodded her understanding. Jonathan could see the disappointment in her eyes, but Cay had been explicitly banned from entering the portal by her parents. She may have entered Hell in her wolf form and saved them all from certain death at Baal's hand, but her mum was not someone you could ignore. In Hobbes End Cay would stay unless told otherwise.

'I'll keep Cay company,' said Elgar, rolling his eyes. 'I'll never hear the end of it if I get to go and she doesn't. I still want to be the first demon to scamper across the divine marble floor of Heaven though.'

Cay smiled at the cat as she bent down to ruffle the fur on his head.

'Mister Stubbs and I will stay here too,' said Montgomery. 'Our job is to protect the village. We'll guard the portal in case things go pear-shaped.' Stubbs nodded in agreement. 'And we can carry on with our snowball fight,' he added.

'Then let's go,' said Jonathan. Waving goodbye to his friends, he entered the portal with Sammael at his side and walked across the plaza. Passing through Heaven's gates, he tried not to look too closely at the scars left behind by Baal's evil. Devastation lay all around them, but bright yellow light shone from above and the stench of ash and decay was now a receding memory. Groups of angels worked to clear rubble and debris from the wide boulevard, and in the distance the great tree at the centre of Heaven stood lifeless yet defiant.

'Where do we start looking?' asked Jonathan.

'I don't know,' replied Sammael. 'Let's keep walking and see what happens.'

They strode onward until they reached the great tree. Jonathan looked up at the lowest branch and a wave of sadness overcame him. It was from this spot that he'd cut down the body of the Archangel Raphael, and so learned the truth about Heaven's fate and Baal's part in it. It was also where he'd first felt the touch of his father's hand after their lives had been torn apart by Belial and his henchmen, Rook, Raven and Crow. The subsequent revelation that his father was already dead still made Jonathan's heart feel like a rock in his chest.

'Come on, come on. Where are you hiding?' said Sammael. She looked about her, desperate to know the source of the strange heartbeat. She didn't have long to wait. The sound rang out like the tolling of a massive bell. It was faster and clearer this time, more urgent.

Thump thump.

Jonathan closed his eyes and concentrated. 'There!' he said. 'It's coming from over there.' He pointed at the one tall building still mostly intact: Raphael's tower.

'Then let's go,' said Sammael, and the pair sprinted off, the soles of their boots drumming on the newly-cleaned marble.

Thump thump.

Jonathan heard the heartbeat again, more recognisable

now, as if it knew that there was someone to hear it, that there was someone coming to help. They came panting to a halt before a plain wooden door at the base of Raphael's tower. It stood unlocked and ajar.

Thump thump.

Sammael rushed into the building. 'That way!' she said, pointing to a spiral staircase built against the outer wall. They raced upward, Jonathan doing his best to follow his great-aunt as they flew across landings, past doors and up flights of stairs, their way lit by sunlight pouring through narrow windows.

Thump thump.

Just as he thought his own heart might burst, the stairs ended and Jonathan found himself on a small landing at the top of the tower. A single wooden door opened into a circular room, filled with the debris of what had once been a library. Shattered wooden bookcases lay heaped against the wall and torn paper littered the floor like confetti. Standing in the centre of the room next to a desk and an upturned chair, Sammael looked about her in desperation.

Jonathan staggered in, bending forward and gripping his knees. He dragged in a raw breath as black spots danced before his eyes. 'Where are we?' he gasped.

'Raphael's study,' said Sammael. 'I thought there would be something here. I thought that Michael might...' She hung her head and shut her eyes, too distressed to speak.

Thump thump. The sound was different this time, less forceful, more hesitant.

'We're on the right track,' said Jonathan. 'We can still hear the heartbeat.'

Sammael nodded. 'I know, but it's getting weaker. We're running out of time. MICHAEL, WHERE ARE YOU?' she bellowed.

Jonathan could feel his own desperation rising to meet that of his great-aunt. It couldn't be a dead end: they must be missing something. Taking a deep breath, Jonathan let go of his panic and looked at the room with an engineer's eyes, with his grandfather's eyes. He could see the way the building was constructed, and there – directly opposite the doorway – was a single block of stone that looked subtly different from all the rest. 'There you are,' he said.

'What is it? What do you see?' said Sammael, her eyes wide and her voice almost pleading.

'I see a secret,' said Jonathan. He walked over to the far wall and pressed his palm against the seemingly-ordinary dressed stone. Without a sound, a section of the wall slid away like a drawn curtain. Behind it, another spiral staircase led upward.

'I think there's another room upstairs, Sam,' said Jonathan. 'This isn't the top of the tower.'

Sammael barged past him and half ran, half clambered up the narrow steps. Jonathan followed close behind her, another faltering *thump thump* ringing in his ears. If this was indeed Michael's heartbeat, then he wasn't going to last much longer.

The stairs ended abruptly, and Jonathan looked up to see the underside of the low dome that formed the pinnacle of Raphael's tower. Light filtered in through slit windows set close to the floor, and in the centre of the room was a large stone plinth. On it lay a burned, scarred wreck of a body. The head was little more than a skull with wisps of hair attached, sightless eye-sockets staring upward and teeth bereft of lips. Shapeless clots of molten glass were fused to the torso and legs, and shattered charcoal protruded from the elbow and knee joints in place of bone.

Jonathan could only stand and watch as Sammael sank to her knees by the body and gently stroked the desiccated cheek.

'Oh, Michael, little brother,' she whispered as tears pattered silently into the dust at her feet.

'So it really is you,' gasped Jonathan. 'How can you still be alive?'

Michael's heartbeat sounded once more, but the gap between thumps grew longer and the sound weaker.

'What do we do, Sam?' asked Jonathan. 'He's dying. I don't really understand why he's not dead, but whatever's keeping him going is about to fail.'

Sammael turned to look at Jonathan, hope stamped all over her face. 'I've got an idea,' she said.

Jonathan couldn't quite believe what he was doing. Inside the cocoon of his manifested wings, he gently cradled the shattered body of Michael as he and Sammael descended the tower and made their way back to the plaza outside Heaven. Angels stopped their repair work to stare in astonishment as the pair raced past, but Sammael ignored them. By the look of intense concentration on her face Jonathan could see that she had something planned, but he had no idea what.

'It needs to be here,' said Sammael as they passed through Heaven's gate and reached the centre of the plaza.

'Why?' asked Jonathan, gently laying Michael's body at their feet.

'If everything goes wrong then we'll cause less damage out here,' she replied.

'What are we going to do?'

'Shed some light on the matter,' said Sammael. 'I don't like the idea of punching yet another hole in reality but I need to open just one more gate.'

'Where to?' asked Jonathan.

'To the star that almost killed him,' said Sammael. 'We need a lot of power if we're going to save his life.'

'But we'll fry!' protested Jonathan.

'I'll protect us from the heat and radiation,' said Sammael. 'You can use the energy. Don't worry. It'll be instinctive for you. Gabriel was a master at fixing things that were broken and you have access to those same skills, even if you don't fully understand them yet.'

Doubt crept up on Jonathan. What if he made a mistake? What if his wings didn't behave themselves? Questions crowded in but he forced himself to be calm, to act as his grandfather would have. There was no time to do anything else.

Sammael stood, spread her arms, and extended a shimmering shield outward from her body until it surrounded Jonathan and Michael. 'Now, gently does it,' she said. Using her newly-restored wings with infinite care, she slowly opened a narrow slit in reality directly above them, right into the heart of a distant star. A column of heat and light slammed down upon them like a hammer and Jonathan cried out in alarm. It took him a few moments to realise that he wasn't being burned to a crisp, even though the light was so bright he could actually see the bones in his fingers.

'Quickly now, Jonathan,' said Sammael. 'Use the sunlight, give it to Michael, your wings are more powerful than you could possibly imagine.'

'But I don't know how,' said Jonathan.

'Yes, deep down you do,' Sammael reassured him. 'Help me heal my brother while I protect us all.'

Jonathan nodded, sweat beading on his brow. He hoped that Sammael was right, now would not be a good time to make a fool of himself. Once again he wove his purple wing ribbons into a cocoon around Michael's shattered body. Without really understanding how, Jonathan felt his wings suck in every ounce of the sun's power that beat down upon him – and give it to Michael. The seconds stretched out into a scorching white eternity as he willed the faltering heartbeat of the ruined angel to keep going.

The pressure grew. The power being funnelled into Michael was extraordinary beyond measure and Jonathan faltered. His wings held enormous strength, but there were limits – and those limits were fast approaching.

'Don't let me be too late!' cried Sammael. 'Don't let him have waited all this time for nothing.'

And then it happened. Something changed: a fever broke, a problem was solved, a broken clock was mended. The gate above him slammed shut and Jonathan slumped to the wonderfully cool marble floor. He lay back as his eyes adjusted to the sudden lack of light and groaned. He felt like he'd been running a marathon across a desert while carrying an anvil.

He turned his head to one side, and with blurry vision saw something that would stay with him for the rest of his life. Lying on the marble next to him was Michael. Not the charred corpse that he'd seen in the tower, but a flesh and blood angel. His body was hairless and his skin was puckered and scarred as if he were recovering from terrible burns, but he was whole and – most importantly – alive.

Sammael kneeled down and gently kissed Jonathan on the forehead. 'Thank you,' she said, gazing at her brother's chest as it rose and fell.

Jonathan turned his head the other way and saw a crowd of astonished faces gathered around the portal to Hobbes End. He smiled at them and they smiled back.

Sammael gazed upon the scarred face of her brother and let out a choked sob as a pair of soft, brown eyes opened to meet her loving gaze. With obvious effort Michael slowly raised his arm, and with fingertips that had felt nothing for centuries he gently brushed the skin of his sister's cheek. Michael smiled.

'I've missed you,' he whispered.

Jonathan sighed with relief. 'We did it,' he said.

From the portal, the rumbling baritone of Kenneth Forrester's voice rolled across the marble of the plaza as he sang out. One by one he was joined by other voices until the whole village was letting Michael, Sammael and Jonathan know how they felt.

'*Amazing Grace, how sweet the sound, that saved a wretch like me, I once was lost, but now am found, was blind, but now I see.*'

Michael smiled once more at his sister, before closing his eyes and letting himself drift away on a sea of song that welcomed him home.

Elgar padded over, and climbed onto Sammael's lap as she kneeled next to her brother, his hand clasped gently in hers.

'I must say,' said the cat, 'that I think Christmas may have come early for you.'

Sammael looked at him, smiled, tipped back her head and laughed until the heavens rang with complete and utter joy.

Chapter 7

The Silk Garden

Flay watched with curiosity as Lilith perched on the edge on her scrying pool. Around him, a small forest of trees were festooned with cobwebs, their branches so thickly covered that little light from Hell's sun could find its way through. Half hidden in the pink-hued gloom, Flay could see movement: sometimes sudden and darting, sometimes slow and deliberate. Lilith's troops attended their mistress with glittering eyes and venom-tipped fangs.

Flay was not afraid of the arachnids that surrounded him; he just didn't like spiders that much. It was the legs that bothered him, all thin and angular and covered with fine hairs, skittering this way and that. Thinking about them lurking in the trees made the back of his neck itch, and he ran his thumb along the edge of his favourite blade to distract himself. It was an old knife, a family heirloom. Passed from father to child, from assassin to assassin, its handle carved from the femur of an angel and its blade forged from the sharpest obsidian. It gleamed dully in the wan light as Flay bounced it in his right hand, testing the weight and balance, indulging himself in the memories of his victories. He had taken many lives with this blade, and after each death he'd cut a small square of skin from his victim to add to his patchwork armour. Made from leather boiled in wax, it fitted his body like a glove, turning him into a ghastly and lethal harlequin. Flay by name, flay by nature.

He sensed more than heard a gentle rustling in the dead leaves above him. Lilith's troops were obedient only to her and they resented his presence. Now one of them seemed to be trying its luck. Flay smiled and closed his eyes. Holding the knife between finger and thumb he sent it flying upward with a lightning smooth flick of his wrist. There was a liquid sound followed by a shrill chittering, and a spider the size of a football dropped to the ground with a squelch as its body split open and spilled greeny-brown goo onto Flay's boots. With a look of contempt, he reached down and pulled his blade free, wiping it clean on the spider's hairy abdomen.

Lilith sighed loudly and turned towards him. 'Please don't upset my children, Flay,' she said. 'I'm trying to concentrate.'

'Then tell your... *children* to play nicely,' said Flay. 'I am not a snack.'

Lilith shook her head and looked about her. There were rustlings from the trees as the spiders that attended her withdrew. 'Better?' she asked.

'Much,' said Flay, regarding her as impassively as ever.

Lilith returned her attention to the pool of water. Ringed with hardened silk, it provided her with a window through which she could observe her enemies. At that moment she had a view of the plaza outside Heaven, seen from the viewpoint of a small spider that scuttled across the marble. She scowled as she watched Michael's resurrection.

'What a pathetic display of sentiment,' snorted Lilith. 'None of it will matter when I'm through, it will just serve to make their despair even greater.'

'So what next in our great game?' asked Flay, idly balancing the tip of his knife on his index finger.

'Now we up the stakes,' said Lilith. She turned to Flay, and even through her veil the look on her face chilled him to the bone.

Chapter 8

A Winter's Tale

Snow was falling on Hobbes End as the sun set behind banks of darkening cloud. Light poured from cottage windows, and Sammael's windmill – its sails still and ice-covered – radiated warmth and welcome. Inside, in a candlelit room, Jonathan and Cay looked at Michael as he lay in bed. Sammael sat next to her brother and watched the resurrected angel's chest rise and fall in a slow and reassuring rhythm. A white sheet covered Michael up to his shoulders, and what skin Jonathan could see was still puckered and scarred.

'How did you manage to bring him back?' whispered Cay. 'I still don't understand how it's possible.'

Jonathan shrugged his shoulders and smiled at her. 'I don't really know,' he said.

Sammael looked at them, the guilt and pain that had been etched into her face since she came back to Hobbes End was gone. In its place was a shining, loving, radiance that revealed her true beauty. Her white hair hung unbound around her shoulders, and her posture spoke of total and utter serenity. She was no longer the *last* Archangel.

'You have no idea what you will one day be capable of, dear boy,' she said to Jonathan. 'To be honest, neither have I, but you will be magnificent. And, as for bringing Michael back, well, every now and again you come across someone whose will to live is so strong they can survive against the odds. My brother's heart is testament to that.' She reached out and placed her hand on Michael's bare arm where it rested on top of the sheets.

'How did he end up hidden in Raphael's tower?' asked Cay.

'I think that when I ignited that last star, the blast threw Michael's body back through the very gate he'd opened to come and find me,' said Sammael. 'Baal was so arrogant he would have assumed that Michael was dead and so just left him there like a trophy. By then Raphael was completely under his control and his plan to frame me for Michael's death had worked, so there was no need to do anything else.'

Cay shuddered. 'Why are Archdemons so horrible?' she said.

'I remember asking Belial the same thing when I fought him,' said Jonathan. 'He said that it was in their nature.'

Sammael snorted in derision. 'In their nature! It's all about choice. You don't have to be a monster if you don't want to be.'

'I hope not,' said Jonathan, still not entirely at ease with his half-angel, half-demon heritage.

'How long do you think Michael will sleep for?' asked Cay.

'As long as he needs to,' said Sammael. 'After all he has suffered, if it takes a year and a day of sitting by his side as he heals then I will be content.' She paused. 'He said that he'd missed me,' she whispered, reaching out to stroke her brother's cheek, 'and I missed him.'

Jonathan felt a lump in his throat. He'd seen that his great-aunt was capable of extraordinary violence, but now he knew that she had much love inside her too. It was wonderful to see.

'Right then,' said Sammael, 'time for dinner. Savantha and Elgar are waiting and they must be famished.' Leaving Michael peacefully asleep, they made their way downstairs and the angel busied herself in the kitchen.

'Can I have a fish finger?' asked Elgar as he stuck his head round the door.

'Once they're cooked,' said Sammael.

'I can wait,' said the cat, eyeing the pack of breadcrumb-covered fishy goodness that sat on the work top, and wondering if he could steal one without her noticing.

'You probably can't,' she said without breaking stride.

'You're scary,' said Elgar.

'Only to bewhiskered thieves,' she replied. 'Now shoo. I

have guests to feed and fish-finger sandwiches are a perfect winter-evening repast.'

His stomach rumbling, Elgar padded through to the lounge where a fire roared cheerfully in a cast-iron stove set against the curved wall. Jonathan, Cay and Savantha sat in comfy chairs and watched the flames behind the glass.

'I love winter,' said Cay. 'Or rather I love it when you're warm and cosy and it's winter outside.' She glanced out of the window where flakes of white drifted past to settle ever deeper on the ground.

'I'm quite looking forward to my first Christmas in Hobbes End,' said Savantha, cradling a mug of tea.

'Do your hands still hurt?' asked Cay.

'A bit,' said Savantha. 'But they heal a little more every day. We all do.'

Jonathan couldn't miss the ever-so-fleeting look of sadness that passed across his mother's face, and he knew that she had thought of his father, Darriel.

'I'm glad,' said Cay. 'How's the piano practice going?'

To Jonathan's surprise, his mother's cheeks reddened. 'It helps a lot,' said Savantha. 'Grimm has been so kind.'

Cay gave Jonathan an unsubtle wink and he rolled his eyes at her total lack of tact or discretion.

'Well, today was a tad busy,' said Elgar, jumping onto the arm of Jonathan's chair. 'We found Michael, got to fight a monster that even Brass is scared of, took a darning needle to the fabric of space and time and even got to do some DIY in Heaven. Not a bad day's work really. I think I've earned my grub.'

'That you have,' said Savantha, smiling at the cat.

They chatted until Sammael arrived with a plate of fish-finger sandwiches. 'Dinner is served,' she said, handing Elgar his own dish.

'Life doesn't get any better than this,' purred the cat, attacking his food with the ferocity of a small panther.

'How's Michael?' Savantha asked, once they'd finished eating.

'He's still sleeping,' said Sammael, 'but he'll recover. He's incredibly strong; he always was. Right now I'm more concerned about that rip that appeared this morning. What I did when we rescued you from Baal's castle... Well... Lucifer was right when he said there'd be consequences. I've damaged the fabric of creation and even the best of carpets will unravel if you cut too many threads. I can only hope that given time the weave will repair itself, as long as we don't hurt it further.'

'Ah, we're more than a match for any squid-monster,' said Elgar, cleaning bits of cod from his whiskers.

Sammael chuckled. 'That we are,' she said. She went quiet and stared at the fire. 'I'm glad you're all here,' she said finally. 'This old windmill felt so empty after Constance grew up and married Ignatius' father, Salvador.'

'Eh?' said Elgar.

Sammael looked puzzled for a moment and then smiled. 'Ah, I haven't told you have I?'

'Told us what?' asked Cay.

'That Ignatius' mother, Constance, is my daughter.'

Elgar coughed out a spray of breadcrumbs. 'She's your daughter!'

'Well, adopted daughter, but that makes no difference to the love I have for her.'

Jonathan smiled at the angel. 'I just remembered something you said when we first met. You said that you'd been listening to Cay and me laugh, and that it... um... warmed your heart?'

'More than you can possibly imagine,' said Sammael. 'For just a little time this windmill was filled with the light that only a child's happiness can bring. I knew what it was like to be a mother, and I was very content.'

'How did you come to adopt Constance?' asked Savantha.

'Ah, therein lies a winter's tale,' said Sammael. 'Would you like to hear it?'

They all nodded.

'It was November 1944 and then, as now, it was snowing,' said Sammael. 'I walked the earth a lot back then, not knowing if I would ever regain my wings. I did my best not to interfere in the affairs of mankind, as the last thing I wanted was to give Hell a reason to start another war. I know Lucifer wouldn't have wanted it but those Archdemons were a different matter, and so I wandered the world and watched. There was beauty and ugliness, cruelty and kindness, mainly in equal measure but sometimes the things I witnessed made me impossibly sad.'

She paused a moment, her eyes distant as she relived a memory. 'It was bitterly cold that winter. An acrid smoke hung low in the air and I was standing on a railway line, next to a cattle truck from which frightened people were being unloaded. I was weeping. I had witnessed death and suffering so many times but nothing on such a brutally efficient scale.'

Jonathan held his breath. He loved history at school, but the mention of cattle trucks made his stomach churn.

'There was one child, one little girl, about five or six years old. She was all alone, and she stumbled on the ramp leading from the train to the ground and fell at the feet of one of the guards. It was the look on his face that did it, his utter contempt as he stared at this little girl. He raised the butt of his rifle to strike her and I stopped him.'

Tears ran down Sammael's cheeks but her voice remained calm. 'I may not have had my wings then but I was still the Morningstar. I shone a light into the darkness of that guard's heart, showed him the truth of what he was doing. I watched the colour drain from his face as realisation struck home. He dropped his rifle and ran screaming into the night. In the confusion I picked up the little girl and walked away into the trees, trying not to think of all the others I had left behind. At every step I took I expected Lucifer to appear and charge me with breaking the truce between Heaven and Hell, but he didn't, and I kept on walking. I barely remember how I got back to England with that little girl held against my chest. I found food and shelter along the way, despite the war that was raging on every side. My world had shrunk to just the two of us, and all I wanted was to get her safely back to Hobbes End.'

'And you did, didn't you?' said Elgar, even his eyes moistening.

'Yeah, I did,' said Sammael. 'I'd called out to Gabriel and he knew we were coming, that little Polish girl and me, my darling Constanzia. My brother was here in this very room when we staggered in. The fire was lit, tea was brewing, food was on the table and he'd even got a bath ready. What a lovely, lovely man he was. After we were washed and fed, I wrapped that little girl in a blanket, sat in my rocking chair, cradled her in my lap and sang to her until she slept.'

Jonathan glanced over at the rocking chair in the corner. He could actually see his great-aunt sitting in it through Gabriel's eyes. The love she felt for the child at that moment so strong it made the very air about her shine.

'Constanzia, or Constance as she eventually became,

didn't speak for almost a year. She was by my side every minute of every day, holding my hand as we walked around the village or picked flowers in the forest. I made her dresses to wear, Gabriel made her toys, but she hated wearing shoes. She seemed to need the feel of grass under her feet as she ran around the village green. She was like a little forest nymph, tiny and delicate, but a survivor nonetheless. When I watched her play I felt closer to happiness than I had been since I was exiled from Heaven. One day – Jonathan, Cay – you'll understand just how extraordinary the unconditional love of a child is. It changes you in ways you couldn't imagine, it softens you, opens you up, lets you see the world around you in a completely different way. And then one day, in the spring of 1946, she went for a swim in the village pond. She'd always been afraid of the water, but she seemed determined to go in anyway. She'd been playing with the gargoyles – who she adored – and decided to walk fully clothed into the water. I ran out of the windmill to call her back, but she just started swimming. I remember sitting there on the edge of the pond, watching her as she doggy-paddled and splashed, and then she laughed. It was the most beautiful sound I had ever heard. She swam towards me, clambered out all dripping wet and, kneeling in front of the gargoyles, she planted a kiss on their foreheads and spoke for the first time.'

'And what did she say?' asked Cay, her eyes wide.

'She said... *Monty*... *Stubbs*...' and then she got up, came over to me where I was sitting, put her arms round my neck and hugged me before whispering in my ear. *Mummy*, she said. And from that moment I was utterly hers.'

'I've got something in my eye,' sniffed Elgar, wiping his face on the arm of the chair.

'Me too,' said Jonathan.

'And so our lives here in Hobbes End carried on as the seasons passed. The world was at peace again, and I watched as my Constance grew into a fine young woman. It was inevitable that she would eventually fall in love, and she couldn't have chosen a better man.'

'Salvador, Ignatius' dad,' said Cay.

'Yes,' said Sammael. 'He was a couple of years younger than her, but they grew up together and by the time they were your age they were inseparable. They were married here at Saint Michael's with Salvador's father Sebastian conducting the service. In time she had a baby and settled into family life at the vicarage. I was so happy for her, but at the same time I felt I had lost my little girl. Without her to care for I went back to feeling guilty about accidentally killing Michael, which as we know now I hadn't, but back then it was all I could think about. I argued with Gabriel and eventually left the village to try and find peace somewhere. I was with Constance at her cottage in Devon when I felt Gabriel die at Belial's hands. It was only then that I realised I had to come home and be the Morningstar again.'

'And now you have your brother back,' said Savantha with a smile.

'Yes, I do,' said Sammael.

There was a moment of quiet before the stillness of the windmill was shattered by an awful, agonised scream.

'Brother!' gasped Sammael as she bolted from her chair and up the stairs to Michael's room. Everyone else ran after her, and Jonathan flew into the bedroom close on his great-aunt's heels.

Michael lay rigid in his bed, his eyes open and a look of horror on his face. Sweat poured from his scarred body and his lips were drawn back in a snarl. His chest heaved as he struggled to draw breath and his hands clawed at the tangled sheets that covered him.

'What is it?' begged Sammael, wrapping her arms round her brother. 'What is it? What are you so afraid of?'

Michael turned to look at her, his eyes flicking wildly from side to side. 'It's coming apart!' he gasped. 'It's all coming apart. Threads... will unravel. So sharp. So, so sharp!'

His body convulsed and his eyes rolled up in his head. With a sigh he sank back into the mattress, unconscious once again. Jonathan shook. What had just happened? Why was the angel so distressed?

Sammael had barely collected her wits when the ghostly figure of Lucifer appeared in the room. He was dressed for battle, his armour rent and pitted and his face blackened by smoke and blood.

'It's happened again,' he said to them all, his voice hollow and echoing as if he were speaking from the bottom of a well. 'Right outside my castle. I can't stop it on my own, Sam. It's too big. I need you and Jonathan. Now!'

There was an awful crash, and a shrill, alien screeching filled their ears. The noise filled them all with dread.

'Hurry, Sam. Please!' begged Lucifer, and then he was gone.

Jonathan looked at his great-aunt with a sinking feeling in his stomach. He remembered the premonition he'd had that very morning, that the peace of the last six months was about to be shattered, and knew in his heart that he'd been right.

Chapter 9

Hellbound

'What do we do?' asked Jonathan.

Sammael looked stricken as she clasped Michael's hand. 'We have to go,' she said. 'Lucifer needs us. He can't close the breach on his own.'

'Cay and I will sit with Michael,' said Savantha. She put her arm round Jonathan's shoulders. 'Be careful, won't you?'

He nodded and kissed her cheek.

'I don't suppose you need my assistance?' Elgar asked Jonathan.

'Not this time, cat,' he said. 'We're going right to the middle of a war zone and I don't think giant squid monsters appreciate sarcasm.'

'Fair point,' said Elgar. 'I'll sit with Michael too then.'

Jonathan nodded. 'You protect everyone while we're gone.'

The cat grinned.

'Grab your coat,' Sammael said to Jonathan. 'We need

to hurry. Keep your fingers crossed this doesn't go pear-shaped.'

She strode off down the stairs and Jonathan almost had to run to keep up. 'This is all my fault,' she said as they left the windmill. 'If I hadn't lost my temper when I killed Baal then none of this would be happening.'

'You didn't know,' said Jonathan. 'And you had every reason to be angry.'

Sammael snorted as they trudged across the snow-covered green. 'I knew exactly what the risks were,' she said angrily. 'I just didn't care. Let's hope we can fix this somehow. I don't want to be the angel responsible for undoing creation.'

Jonathan didn't know how to respond. He wanted to make his great-aunt feel better somehow but couldn't find the words. When she got in one her black moods there was no reasoning with her. No wonder she fell out with Gabriel, Jonathan thought to himself.

'How do we get to Lucifer in time?' Jonathan asked. 'It'll take too long if we use the tunnel to Hell from the plaza outside Heaven.'

'I'm going to redirect the portal so it points at Lucifer's castle,' said Sammael. 'I don't want to start opening up any new holes. If I move one that's already there it shouldn't cause any more damage.'

Jonathan nodded, but his knowledge of portals was still in

its infancy. He understood the concept but he was a long way from ever trying to open one himself. They arrived and, while snow gathered in their hair, Sammael summoned her wings and framed the opening to Heaven with gloss-black ribbons.

'Watch what I'm doing,' she said, a little too sharply. 'It's just a question of knowing where you want to move the opening to. I'm familiar with the area around Lucifer's castle so this shouldn't be too difficult.'

Jonathan nodded, trying his best to follow what Sammael was doing. He sensed rather than saw the tips of her wing ribbons grip the edges of reality. The plaza outside Heaven disappeared as the angel turned slowly to her left, taking the portal with her. Jonathan felt dizzy as the view inside it spun crazily. It was like watching a slide show at high speed through a telescope.

'Gotcha!' said Sammael triumphantly.

The portal stopped spinning and locked on to a new location: a hillside overlooking a grassy plain. In the centre, on an island in the middle of a swift-flowing river, a heavily fortified castle towered above everything. At its base, all hell was breaking loose, literally.

A small army, with Lucifer at its head, was ranged in a semicircle around a huge rip. It must have been at least twenty metres high, and it was getting bigger as something vast and utterly terrifying forced its way through and into Hell itself.

'Oh...' said Jonathan. 'Now I get why Lucifer was in a panic.'

'Oh God,' gasped Sammael. 'We need to get down there now. Run!'

Forcing his reluctant legs into a sprint, Jonathan dashed after the angel. The *baby* creature he'd seen that morning had been enough to make him want to wet his pants, but this was another matter entirely. The monster that was clawing its way into this reality was so hideous it was almost beyond description. It kept changing form as if it couldn't make up its mind how terrifying it wanted to be. It was a massive, amorphous blob upon which gaping, fang-filled mouths kept appearing and disappearing at random. There were tentacles, clusters of eyes, dripping goo that burned everything it touched, but worst of all was the sheer malevolence the thing radiated. Its hate for this world, this creation, was so strong it was like running into a wall of loathing.

Jonathan faltered in his stride for a moment and Sammael turned round to grab his arm. 'This is no time for fear,' she said, lightning flashing in her eyes. 'Feel it, yes, but master it too. Remember what you are, what you are capable of. You are the grandson of Gabriel Artificer and you will not let him down!'

Taken aback by the force of Sammael's words, Jonathan could only nod. He took a deep breath and continued his sprint down the hill, across the plain and towards the nightmare that threatened the fabric of creation itself.

Lucifer's army was composed of demons of all shapes and sizes. There was a time when Jonathan would have been frightened of their strangeness, but compared to what they were fighting it was nothing. Among the demons Jonathan could also see angels, dressed in black battle armour emblazoned with a white star. Some of them had stayed behind, he thought to himself as he ran. Even after Heaven was safe, some of the angels Lucifer had saved from Baal's scheming had chosen to stay with him, to fight at his side. And fight they did; the area in front of the rip was littered with bodies as the vast tentacles, pseudopods and gnashing teeth wreaked havoc among the ranks of the defenders. Lucifer launched bolt after bolt of searing fire at the monster, but all they seemed to do was annoy it. For every tentacle that was sheared off or burned away, another grew even bigger in its place.

'That thing is huge,' said Sammael, as they drew nearer. 'We need to drive it back somehow or we'll never be able to close the rip, the edges are too far apart.'

Jonathan had no idea what they should do. He almost wished Elgar had come along after all. Some biting sarcasm would have been a welcome distraction. The din of battle grew louder, with screams, shouts and the unearthly hissing and shrieking of the monster from outside of space and time.

'Down!' shouted Sammael, as the tip of a flailing tentacle whipped over their heads like a steel cable. Jonathan ducked, buffeted by the force of the narrow miss. The stench of the thing was appalling: an acrid mix of acid and rot that made him want to gag. The only good thing about the scenario was that the creature's bulk blocked the rip so tightly, air wasn't being sucked out into the void beyond, and all of them with it. A sudden thought made Jonathan's heart sink even further.

'We're going to have to time this right,' he gasped. 'If we push that thing back we're not going to have time to seal the breach before we're all sucked into whatever lies on the other side!'

'Yes,' said Sammael. 'I know. Come on, let's get to Lucifer.'

Jonathan looked ahead and spotted the fallen angel right in the thick of it, bellowing orders left, right and centre. Arrows filled the air, peppering the creature with feathered shafts but doing little actual damage. There was a thump and a whistling sound from above him, and Jonathan saw a bolt the size of a small tree trunk fly from a ballista mounted on the wall surrounding the castle. Its barbed steel tip glinted in the sunlight as it struck the creature right in one of its unblinking eyes. The bolt buried itself deeply and the eye ruptured with a sickly pop.

Enraged, the creature gave a deafening bellow and redoubled its attacks, its acid-covered tentacles slamming to the ground and crushing anyone too slow to get out of the way. Corrosive ichor splashed everywhere and demons and angels alike screamed as it burned through their armour.

'Do something!' bellowed Lucifer as he spotted Jonathan and Sammael running towards him.

'We need to push it back,' shouted Sammael.

'I'm well aware of that,' said Lucifer. 'What do you think I'm trying to do!' He launched yet another fireball from his hands and it struck the creature full on, burning its way deeply into the shuddering mass.

By Lucifer's side Albert stood at the ready, a massive iron maul gripped in his hands and a grim look on his face. Every time a tentacle came too close, he swung the club with extraordinary speed, swatting away the attacks with no apparent effort. Drops of acid spattered across his body, leaving smoking rents as they burned their way into his metal frame.

'I need to get above that thing,' said Sammael, a wild look in her eyes. 'Start stitching the edges together. You need to keep it off me.'

'I'll do my best,' said Lucifer. 'Jonathan, stand here by my side. Use those wings of yours to help Albert.'

Jonathan nodded, unsure how much help he could be. He didn't know how to throw bolts of fire, or anything else for that matter. The creature was just so... massive. How would his wings be able to stop it if it suddenly decided to advance?

'Be brave,' said Sammael, kissing him on the forehead before manifesting her own wings and shooting up into the sky. Once more Jonathan was reminded of how powerful his great-aunt was. He remembered what she had done to Baal, incinerating the Archdemon's body before flinging what was left of his evil soul into the chaos the monster in front of him called home. But this thing was too big for her to do that, and deep down Jonathan knew that Sammael was afraid of causing yet more damage. This time her power and her will would be bent towards repair, not destruction.

'Right then,' growled Lucifer. 'Let's be having you.' Focusing all his rage, he launched bolt after bolt of fire at the creature, trying to get its full attention; in this he was quite successful. Jonathan stared in terror as myriad eyes swivelled their way, slavering mouths gaped and every tentacle the thing had at its disposal lashed forward at the same time.

Jonathan did the only thing he knew how. He manifested his wings and threw them up in front of him, hoping they would protect Lucifer and Albert – and anyone else who was nearby – from the impact.

The ground heaved, the world spun, and Jonathan was knocked off his feet as three tentacles crashed down on them from above. He fully expected to be flattened, but watched in astonishment as those magnificent purple ribbons did their stuff. They fanned out into a vast arc, and between them crackled a kaleidoscope of coloured symbols, just like the ones that flowed through the gates of Heaven. The tentacles struck the barrier with appalling force, and yet it held. Jonathan grunted with effort, and bared his teeth in a fierce grin as the creature screamed out in pain and recoiled. He could see that where the tentacles had struck his wings, they burned.

'Hah!' laughed Lucifer, pulling Jonathan to his feet. 'That'll teach it some manners.'

'What did I just do?' asked Jonathan. 'Why is it pulling back?'

'It's your wings, boy. It's your wings,' said Lucifer triumphantly. 'Just like Sammael's they're the stuff of creation itself: starlight, order, warmth, love, snips and snails and puppy dog's tails; the whole shebang. That thing is pure anti-life, cold, black, roiling chaos. You're everything it isn't and it hates it.'

He gripped Jonathan by the shoulders and looked up at the serrated purple ribbons as they filled the air above them. 'Oh God, I miss having wings like those at my command. Mine were so white it was blinding.'

A look of terrible sadness flickered across the fallen angel's face. 'Still, enough talk. Look, Sammael is in position and we need to press forward.'

78

Tipping back his head Lucifer called out to his troops. 'ADVANCE!' As one, they roared in agreement and threw themselves into the fray with renewed vigour. Seeing that the army was on the move, Sammael positioned herself directly above the rip, hanging motionless in the air with her wings outspread. She concentrated, trying to shut out the din from the battle below as she gently probed the top of the rip with her ribbons.

The damage was immense compared to the one she'd already mended, and that one hadn't had an alien beast the size of an office block trying to push its way through at the same time. Fighting off her uncertainty, Sammael carefully fed her will and power into the frayed tatters of reality, priming the edges to knit together. Sweat poured down her face and her body shook with the effort, but there was no other way; she had to fix this or all was lost. And then she had it, the creature was recoiling from Jonathan just enough for her to feel the pressure easing. Gathering all her strength she began to pull the glowing edges of the rip towards each other.

With a roar of pain the creature thrashed mindlessly as the atom-thin border between our world and the void bit into its hide. Black, corrosive ichor spurted from the wound, and Sammael grunted at the resistance caused by the alien's body. It was like trying to cut through stale cheese with a plastic knife.

Jonathan watched his great-aunt in awe. He could feel her efforts and saw they were being rewarded. The rip slowly closed on the creature and, trapped in a sharp-edged vice, it wailed and tried to heave itself backward, but it was too late. Unable to move and slowly being cut in half, it gave up on escape and focused all its efforts on one last burst of carnage. As it flailed at the advancing army, a single eye on its back caught sight of Sammael where she hung above it. Before anyone could shout a warning it raised a single, massive tentacle, gathered its strength and swatted her from the air like a fly.

'No!' Jonathan screamed, as Sammael's limp body tumbled across the sky to land with a sickening thump by the castle wall. Jonathan held his breath, his stomach churning with hope, but Sammael lay still as death, her body twisted and smoking.

'Jonathan!' cried Lucifer, his face pale and grim.

He turned to the fallen angel and saw what Lucifer was looking at. It wasn't the fallen body of his great-aunt, but the creature. Finally rid of its tormentor it opened every mouth it had and screamed utter hatred at them all. Radiating malice so strong it made the air shudder, it threw itself towards them, a vast mass of gnashing teeth, crushing tentacles and corrosive acid.

Chapter 10

Learning to Fly

Jonathan stood rooted to the spot as the creature slithered its way forward, crashing against the front ranks of the army and batting them aside as if they weren't there.

'Snap out of it and go and close that rip!' Lucifer screamed.

Too shocked to respond Jonathan gaped at him; Sammael could be dead and Lucifer was asking him to do the impossible. 'But I don't know how to fly yet!' he said. 'Sam's been trying to teach me but it's so difficult.'

'Stop with the excuses,' said Lucifer. 'It's in your blood, your bones, your flipping soul. Stop thinking about it and just do it!'

Panic gripped Jonathan. He really had no idea how to use his wings to fly. He'd read about it in the library in his head, but translating the theory into actual flight was a different matter. His wings were unique – the mix of angelic and demonic genes saw to that – and therein lay the problem; they didn't work in the same way as Sammael's and it confused him.

'We're running out of time,' Lucifer shouted. 'We'll all die unless you close that rip! I'll distract that creature even if I have to let it eat me...' The fallen angel suddenly grinned. 'Oh, I've just had such a good idea. Please, Jonathan, trust your instincts, ask Gabriel, do whatever you have to do but get up there and get knitting.'

Jonathan nodded, desperate to assist but so afraid that he would fail. There, in the midst of all the smoke and the screaming, he asked his grandfather for help. He put every ounce of feeling he had into the request, every fear, every hope. He asked, not for himself, but for all those who were fighting and dying around him. He asked on behalf of Sammael where she lay broken on the ground, he asked on behalf of Cay, Elgar, the gargoyles and Hobbes End, he asked on behalf of creation itself, and Gabriel answered him.

The words that had echoed through Jonathan's mind when he'd first absorbed Gabriel's knowledge sang to him once again in his grandfather's voice. '*Now Grandson, let me show you what it's like to fly – what it's like to slip the surly bonds of earth and touch the face of God.*'

When he'd faced and defeated Belial, it had been Gabriel in the driving seat, a last gift from the old angel before his soul moved on, but this time was different. Jonathan still didn't understand the mechanics, but chose to let himself be guided by the knowledge inside his head. He could feel the essence of everything that Gabriel had been running though his veins, and it was glorious.

Without effort, the black glass armour he had worn into battle against both Belial and Baal shimmered into being, his ribbons swept downward like the wings of a hawk and he shot into the sky. He dived towards the creature, knowing that it could see him coming. Tentacles whipped towards him, but as each one drew close he smashed it away with his wings. His armour smoked with acid burns, but he made the creature pay by visiting extraordinary suffering upon it. The thing ceased its forward motion but refused to retreat. It hunkered down and took every ounce of punishment that Jonathan and Lucifer's army could inflict, while dishing out plenty of its own. It was a stalemate and Jonathan knew it. While those tentacles were waving about he would never be able to concentrate enough to close the rip without ending up like poor Sammael.

'Now would be the time for your good idea!' he shouted to Lucifer far below.

The fallen angel nodded and turned to Albert, whispering in the construct's ear. 'I'm so sorry,' said Lucifer when he'd finished explaining his plan. Albert looked downcast for a moment, and Lucifer felt a pang of sadness for the sturdy golem. 'It is necessary, but you will not be forgotten. I promise you that.'

Albert nodded his agreement, opening his arms wide so

that Lucifer could touch his chest. Using every ounce of power he had left, the fallen angel filled Albert with liquid fire. Every bolt of flame that Lucifer might have launched at the creature he now gave to the construct, and Albert began to glow. First it was a dull red, then yellow like the sun, and finally white like burning snow. Albert shook with the power contained inside him.

'Now RUN, my friend!' bellowed Lucifer. 'Run and be immortal.'

The construct – who had seemed so slow and lumbering – sprinted across the battlefield and right at the creature where it writhed and flailed. Albert aimed himself towards the biggest open mouth, and before the thing could register what was happening, he ran straight inside it.

There was a sudden lull in the battle as the creature paused, a look of alien surprise on its distorted features, and then Albert, forged from demon weaponry and given life by Lucifer himself, exploded with colossal force.

The creature screamed in agony and wrapped its tentacles round its body as smoke poured from every mouth.

'Now, Jonathan!' shouted Lucifer.

Not needing to be asked twice, Jonathan positioned himself above the rip and gently inserted his wing ribbons into the fabric of creation. He'd seen and felt Sammael make the repair that morning and hoped he could repeat what she had done. It was as if his consciousness jumped sideways into a world of pure mathematics. Symbols flowed around and through him as he saw how creation was knitted together with such astonishing complexity. At his feet the rip felt like an open wound, and Jonathan finally understood just how much of a threat it was. He could feel the very fabric of reality writhing in pain, and knew that he had to fix it, and quickly.

Just as Sammael had done, he sent his will along the tattered edges of the weave, gently encouraging them to seek the threads from which they had been severed. Jonathan once again felt an odd sensation of wrongness wash over him. He couldn't concentrate enough to figure out what it was, but once this was finished he promised himself that he would get to the bottom of it.

With every broken thread under his control, he asked the edges of the rip to meet each other, funnelling all the power of his wings into the weave. It responded joyfully, and began to close once again.

Caught in the jaws of the healing rip, the creature shook with a mixture of fear and rage. Jonathan could sense it was badly wounded, but it still had enough strength for one last blow. It uncoiled a single tentacle from its shattered body and sent it flying upwards in a wide arc. Jonathan could feel it coming, but if he let go now then everything would be lost; he had to finish the job no matter what. Abandoning all finesse, he heaved on his wing ribbons and pulled the edges of the rip together with the force of a guillotine blade.

Reality slammed shut, cutting the creature in half with an awful squelch as the threads of creation wove themselves back together. Jonathan succeeded just as the still-moving tentacle struck him a terrific blow. Swatted from the sky in the same manner as Sammael, he dimly felt himself falling before everything went black.

'Well, I must say that was quite the show,' nodded Flay as he gazed into Lilith's scrying pool, a spider sitting on the battlements of Lucifer's castle providing them with a grandstand view.

'Wasn't it just,' she said, smiling behind her veil. 'I think that should be enough to give Lucifer the nudge he needs.'

'Let's hope so,' said Flay. 'They almost didn't stop it. I for one don't wish to end up being digested inside one of those... things.'

'Oh, Flay,' said Lilith. 'Where's your spine?'

'Between my skull and my pelvis,' replied Flay. 'And that's where I'd like it to stay.' He paused. 'That boy, he really is quite powerful isn't he.'

'Yes,' said Lilith. 'I think you'll probably have to kill him. Add another... trophy to that armour of yours. He is the only one of his kind after all; I would have thought that despatching him would give you great satisfaction.'

Flay grinned, but there was no mirth in his face, only a cold, cold hunger for a challenge worthy of his name.

Lilith stroked Michael's Spear where it lay in her lap and it sang to her: a ballad of pain and rage, knowing it was being corrupted but being unable to do anything about it. It was slave to her will now, and that was that.

'What next?' asked Flay.

'We watch and wait,' said Lilith happily. 'We watch and wait.'

'Jonathan?' said a strangely familiar voice. 'Jonathan, can you hear me?'

'What?' he groaned, feeling like he'd been hit by a bus. Every bit of him hurt, even his eyelashes.

'He's awake,' the voice called out, and Jonathan could hear footsteps approaching, boots click-clacking on a wooden floor.

'Jonathan?' said Savantha. 'Are you OK?'

He almost burst into tears at the sound of her voice. 'Hi, Mum,' he said.

'I'm very proud of you, my brave boy,' said Savantha, gently running a hand over Jonathan's brow. 'Thank you for not getting yourself killed.'

He reached up and squeezed her hand. 'What about Sam?' he asked, fully expecting to be told that his great-aunt was dead.

'I'm very hard to bump off,' the angel said from nearby. 'We appear to be sharing the same hospital room.'

'Sammael is swathed in bandages and looks like a mummy,' said Savantha, 'but she's going to be fine.'

'I don't feel like it,' said Sammael with a groan. 'Someone get me a glass of water with a straw, I don't think I can move my head yet.'

'I'll fetch it,' said the other voice.

It took Jonathan a moment but then he remembered where he'd heard it before. Elgar's older brother had been sitting under a tree in Hell, eating a sandwich and nursing a broken leg. Unlike Elgar, he'd been spared the punishment of being turned into a cat by the Archdemon Belial. 'Delius?' said Jonathan. 'Is that you?'

'Yep,' said Delius. 'I went and fetched your mum after you were brought in.'

'And me,' said Elgar, jumping onto Jonathan's bed.

'And me!' said Cay as she rushed into the room.

'Anyone else?' said Jonathan with a chuckle; wincing at the pain it caused his ribs. He opened his eyes and it took them a moment to focus on the room around him. 'Where are we?' he asked.

'My castle,' said Lucifer, from where he was standing by a large, arched window on the far side of the room. 'You did well, very well. I'm impressed, and I don't say that often, or indeed, at all.'

Sammael gave a snort from where she lay in her bed. Jonathan looked over and saw that his mother was right; his great-aunt was swathed head to foot in bandages. 'You do look like a mummy.'

'Cheers,' she said. 'I got a face-full of that horrible acid. I'll take a dip in the pond when I get back to the village. It's good for the complexion.'

Jonathan nodded. The pond water had eased the burns Sammael received when they'd fought Baal. 'I take it the creature from the black lagoon is resting in peace?' he asked.

'Pieces, to be accurate,' said Lucifer, trying not to smile. 'I'm going to have a deuce of a job to clear up the mess though. I can't just leave that decomposing, bisected carcass outside my front door, the smell will be terrible.' He looked out of the window and sighed heavily. 'I'll miss Albert. I'd grown quite attached to him, but he did make quite a good bomb.'

Jonathan nodded. Albert may have been a construct, just like Brass, Monty and Stubbs, but he'd been sentient all the same. His sacrifice shouldn't be forgotten.

'There must be some bits of him left,' pondered Lucifer, 'although I'll have to search through tons of alien goo to find them. Delius, perhaps you would be so kind as to...'

'Hell no!' said Delius. 'I'm a librarian, not a zoologist.'

'Just a thought,' said Lucifer. 'Anyway, I think we all need to have a chat. This sort of thing can't be allowed to continue. Jonathan, I lost almost a quarter of my army battling that thing. If you and Sammael hadn't got here when you did, we'd all be dead and reality would be crumbling around our ears. That is not something I'll tolerate.'

'This is all my fault,' said Sammael. 'If I hadn't...'

'And you can stop that as well!' barked Lucifer. 'You lost your temper with Baal, and quite frankly he deserved it. Stop feeling so guilty about everything.'

'OK,' whispered Sammael, not wanting to incur Lucifer's ire while she was trussed up in gauze.

'Ooooooh! Someone got out of the wrong side of bed this morning,' said Elgar.

Savantha laughed. 'He's right, you know,' she said to Lucifer as he stood by the window, fuming silently.

'If Belial's curse hadn't already turned you from a demon boy into a cat, Elgar, I'd seriously consider doing it myself,' Lucifer growled. 'Look, I've been pondering what to do and I can only think of one option. It's something I'd never consider unless the entire universe was at stake but I don't think we have a choice.'

'And what is this cunning plan?' asked Elgar.

'We heal the weave of creation, all of it, at the same time.'

There was a stunned silence.

'Well, you're a tough audience,' said Lucifer. 'I was hoping for a bit more enthusiasm.'

'How on earth would we do that?' asked Jonathan.

'I think I know,' said Sammael. 'There's only one thing with the power to do that, and it's so dangerous that nobody would ever think of using it. That's why it's been safely hidden away for a very long time.'

'So you know where it is then?' asked Lucifer.

'Yes,' said Sammael. 'Until today I wouldn't have believed it would ever be needed, but I agree that we may not have the choice.'

'Glad we're thinking along the same lines,' said Lucifer.

'Will someone please explain what you're talking about?' said Cay. 'What is this super-dangerous thingy you want to use to fix everything?'

'It's a book,' said Sammael. 'No, it's *the* book: the book of creation. It's only got one page in it, but that's all you need.'

Jonathan remembered the story Sammael had told him when she first arrived in Hobbes End, the story of how the universe was created. Lucifer had done it, he'd been given the words to read and the big bang had followed, bringing light and life to empty chaos.

'It is the book you read from, isn't it?' said Jonathan. 'Right at the beginning when there was just you.'

'Yep,' said Lucifer. 'I can't read the words again, nobody can. If that was to happen we'd end up creating another universe inside this one, and that would be... messy. I just need the book itself. It's so powerful that I may, and I stress the word *may*, be able to use it to fix all this damage without hitting the cosmic delete button.'

'And if you screw up?' asked Elgar.

'Then I wouldn't bother booking a summer holiday,' said Lucifer.

'Oh...' said the cat.

'So where is the book, Sam?' asked Lucifer.

Sammael sighed.

Lucifer raised his eyebrows in expectation. 'Well?'

'It's buried with Uriel in Heaven, inside a tomb built to honour his sacrifice and preserve his body for all time.'

'Makes sense,' said Lucifer. 'Right then, do you think anyone will mind if we open the tomb and borrow it?'

Listening in to the conversation from the safety of the scrying pool, Lilith allowed herself a satisfied smile.

'Well now, isn't that nice,' she gloated. 'So that's where the book is. And not only that, I think they're going to fetch it for me too. How frightfully helpful.'

'I must admit I wasn't sure if they would take the bait,' said Flay. 'I stand corrected.'

'Never underestimate the power of planning ahead,' said Lilith. 'With the spear and the book in my hands I will be unstoppable. A new day is dawning, Flay, and the only Morningstar in the sky will be me!'

Chapter 11

Michael

Jonathan walked stiffly into Lucifer's study. He could sense his body mending itself, but he still felt as though he'd been hit by a bus.

'Ah, there you are,' said Lucifer. 'What do you think of the décor?'

Jonathan couldn't miss the large, scaly hearthrug or the familiar reptilian head mounted on a plaque on the chimney breast. 'Belial looks... surprised,' said Jonathan.

'Understandable given the circumstances of his demise,' said Lucifer, raising an eyebrow. 'Still, it amuses me when I'm sitting here of an evening doing the crossword. Anyhow, that's not why I asked to see you.'

'What do you want to talk about?' asked Jonathan.

'First, I wanted to say how pleased I was that you found Michael and brought him back from the brink of death. Sam filled me in on the details while you were asleep. It means much to her to have her brother back.'

'Yeah,' said Jonathan. 'I've never seen her so happy.

Mum's gone back to the windmill to keep an eye on Michael now she knows I'm OK.'

Lucifer nodded. 'Still, I'm not a believer in coincidence. Don't you find it curious that Michael chooses to call out for help at the same time as these rips start appearing?'

'I hadn't thought of that,' said Jonathan. 'Do you think the two are connected somehow?'

'Maybe,' said Lucifer, 'but that's a mystery for another day. Right now we need to concentrate on recovering the book of creation. I want you to understand exactly what it is, and how earth-shatteringly dangerous it can be.'

'I kinda got that already,' said Jonathan.

'That's as maybe but I'm going to hammer the point home,' said Lucifer. 'It may look like a book, but it's not really. It's a container for forces that are so primal, so powerful, that locking it away after it was used was the only sensible thing to do.'

'I guess Heaven wanted to keep it away from you after you started that civil war,' said Jonathan, unafraid to speak the truth.

'Exactly,' said Lucifer. 'Burying it with Uriel, the last of the Araelim – the first angels to be created after me – was only fitting. What I don't know is how difficult it's going to be to retrieve it. It was sealed away by a master engineer after all.'

Jonathan blinked. 'You mean Gabriel?'

'Exactly,' said Lucifer. 'Your grandfather was young then, and at the height of his powers. Of the four siblings he was the one I respected – and feared – the most. He understood the nature of things, he saw the big picture, and that made him very cautious. He will not have made it easy for anyone to get hold of that book. At the time he would have wanted to keep it out of my hands most of all.'

'Now you know where it is, why don't you just go and get it?' said Jonathan.

'I can't,' said Lucifer. 'Like I said, Gabriel made sure that it would be safe. Sam informs me that only someone of his bloodline can open the door to the tomb, which narrows the field down to three people; only one of whom can currently walk.'

'You mean me?' said Jonathan. 'You want me to go and fetch it for you?'

'Does that bother you?' asked Lucifer. 'Do you distrust my intentions?'

Jonathan paused for a moment. Over the last few months he'd seen what Lucifer was capable of, but the fallen angel's actions had demonstrated that he just wanted everything to be peaceful and tick along nicely. He'd read the universe into being after all, and as he had been with the gates of Heaven, Lucifer seemed to be particularly possessive about things he'd helped create.

'I trust you,' said Jonathan.

Lucifer smiled at him, and for once he showed a flicker of genuine warmth. 'I meant what I said when we first met, Jonathan. I didn't think your existence was possible, and yet here you are, fighting at my side to hold things together and protect the ones you love. You give me hope.'

'Hope for what?' asked Jonathan, wondering what was going through the fallen angel's head.

'Hope for the future,' Lucifer replied. 'A future where I can retire, put my feet up and entrust the custody of this fragile creation to someone who has the power, the will, and the heart to look after it with as much passion as I.'

'You mean me?' said Jonathan, blinking in surprise.

'Well, I don't mean Elgar,' said Lucifer, 'endearingly blunt as he is. Everything changes, Jonathan, nothing lasts for ever as Gabriel well knew. The time of Heaven and Hell being separate is coming to an end, you are living proof of that. There will come a moment when I, Sam, and now Michael will want to take a back seat and enjoy some fly fishing, or something equally relaxing. It'll be your time, my boy, and you need to be ready for it.'

Jonathan sighed. During the last year his entire world had been tipped upside-down in unimaginable ways, and now Lucifer was telling him that he would eventually be in charge... of everything.

'Don't fret though,' said Lucifer, seeing the troubled look on Jonathan's face. 'There's a long road between now and then and, if you are to build something magnificent we need to fix creation right now, or there'll be nothing left for you to care for.'

Jonathan nodded, knowing what Lucifer said was true. What they faced affected every angel, every demon, every human. It could not be ignored.

'Anyway, the book,' said Lucifer. 'It doesn't contain words as such, just a single equation, a string of quantum mathematics: the language of creation itself. It takes great skill and power to read, but in doing so you unleash forces that can either create or destroy. It's the big bang in a limited-edition hardback.'

'Oh,' said Jonathan.

'So whatever you do, don't open it and don't try to read it. Only I can use the power of that book to help us, without erasing the universe by accident.'

'Are you sure you'll be able to do it?' Jonathan asked.

'Nope,' said Lucifer. 'But what choice do we have? Reality is fraying at the seams and these rips will keep on appearing. It's only a matter of time before we can't stop them. Sometimes you can't keep darning an old pair of socks, you have to go and get a new pair instead. Anyhow, we can't wait for Sammael or Michael to be well enough to go on an expedition, so you're it. Go and get that book, then maybe we can all put our feet up for a bit, have a picnic or something.'

'OK,' said Jonathan. 'I guess I'll see you when I get back.'

'You'll be fine,' said Lucifer. 'It's not as if you're going anywhere dangerous.'

Jonathan nodded and left the room, although he didn't entirely share Lucifer's confidence. If there was one thing experience had taught him, it was that danger often lurked in the most unlikely places.

'Even my bruises have bruises,' said Sammael, perched on the edge of her bed. She'd been de-mummified and was back in her usual black dress, but she looked as though she'd picked a fight with a steamroller, and lost badly. One side of her face was terribly burned and patches of her hair were missing.

'You look awful,' said Elgar.

'Thanks,' said Sammael, getting slowly to her feet.

Jonathan walked in and saw his great-aunt was ready to leave. 'How are you feeling?' he asked her.

'Delicate,' she replied. 'Apparently my appearance will scare small children.' She glared at the cat.

'I was just being honest,' said Elgar. 'Right then, shall we go? I've had Mum bending my ear all morning about the fact she still has a cat for a son. She'd quite like me to be a boy again, but there's the small problem of Belial being unable to remove his curse, given that he's dead and all. Still, I've promised to write more, so my parents are less irritated than they were with my lack of communication.'

'I struggle to believe that they could be *more* irritated with you,' said Sammael, trying to smile but wincing when it pulled on her burned skin.

'I guess we should be off,' said Jonathan. 'I've got to fetch this book.'

Sammael nodded. 'I'll need a few hours to recharge. Hopefully by then I'll have enough juice to shift the portal back to Heaven without breaking myself utterly.'

'You will,' said Jonathan, happy to have Sammael in one piece.

They left Lucifer's castle and trudged slowly up the hill, Jonathan supporting his great-aunt. Behind them, hundreds of figures were busy dismembering the body of the creature and carting off the bits to be burned on huge pyres. The smell was awful.

'I'm going to start calling you Slasher Smith after what you did to that thing,' said Elgar.

'Please don't,' said Jonathan as they re-entered Hobbes End. Brass and the gargoyles were guarding the portal, and beamed at them as they came through.

'Welcome back,' said Stubbs. 'Nice job with tentacle-boy. Couldn't have done it better myself.'

'Thanks,' said Jonathan. He was about to ask if all had been quiet in his absence when he heard his mother calling from the door to the windmill.

'Jonathan, Sam, come quickly. It's Michael!'

'Is he having another seizure?' cried Sammael, limping towards her home as fast as she could.

'No,' Savantha called back, a huge smile on her face. 'He's awake, and he's asking for you.'

They burst into Michael's room to find him propped up against a mountain of pillows and talking to Cay who gave Sammael a huge smile and stood up so the angel could have her chair.

'Brother?' said Sammael, as she sat down.

'You look like you've been in the wars,' he said, his brown eyes taking in her injuries. 'That's normally my job.'

She reached out and squeezed his hand. 'Are you OK?'

'Given that I spent several centuries as a blackened corpse on the edge of death, I'd say I was bearing up rather well.' He laughed, and the sound brought tears to his sister's eyes.

Michael rubbed his chin and scalp. 'I think my hair is actually starting to grow back, which is nice. I look odd without eyebrows.' He turned his attention to Jonathan. 'Come here,' said Michael. 'I want to meet Gabriel's grandson, the impossible boy. Cay and Savantha have been filling me in on what's happened in my absence.'

Jonathan perched on the edge of the bed. Michael extended his hand and Jonathan took it. The angel's grip was firm; his body was repairing itself, slowly filling with the strength for which Michael had been legendary.

'Thank you for listening when I called out to you,' said Michael. 'I didn't know if you would hear me.'

'There's no mistaking that heart of yours,' said Sammael.

Michael grinned. 'I had so little energy left. If you hadn't found me when you did then I would have been gone for good.'

'Why did you choose that moment to call to us?' asked Jonathan.

Michael frowned. 'It's difficult to explain,' he said. 'I wasn't really aware of anything when I was, to all intents and purposes, dead, but I had this overwhelming sense that something terrible was happening, something connected to me, and that I needed to reach out.'

Jonathan frowned as he remembered what Lucifer had said. Were Michael and the rips in reality connected? And if so, how?

'All that matters is that you are here, little brother,' said Sammael, her face alight with happiness.

'Good trick with the sunlight,' said Michael. 'Nothing like being force-fed ultraviolet radiation to perk you up. Have you got any food? I'm starving.'

'I'll get you some soup,' said Sammael, getting up from her chair.

'Soup!' said Michael. 'I was hoping for a sandwich the size of a stack of books.'

'One step at a time, little brother,' said Sammael as she reached the door.

'Oh, Sam,' said Michael.

'Yes?'

'My almost-death. It wasn't your fault.'

'I know, Michael,' she replied, all traces of guilt gone from her face. 'I know.'

'So then, Jonathan,' said Michael, once his sister had gone downstairs. 'I gather Lucifer is now on our side and we're two Archdemons down. Quite the effect you seem to be having on the world I knew.'

'Well, you know,' shrugged Jonathan. 'All in a day's work.'

'That's my boy.' The angel laughed, clapping Jonathan on the shoulder and almost knocking him off the bed. 'It's good to be back. I just wish I knew what happened to my spear, my right hand feels empty without it. It's probably floating somewhere between the stars never to be seen again. I could ask Sam to make me another one I suppose, but without Gabriel to help her it just wouldn't be the same weapon.'

'Maybe I could do something?' said Jonathan. 'It's going to take me a while to understand Gabriel's knowledge, but one day.'

'Oh yes, my brother's parting gift to you. Cay mentioned that.' Michael went silent, sadness overcoming him. 'Did he... did Gabriel... Did he die well?'

Jonathan felt his own sadness at his grandfather's passing

well up. 'He saved us in the end,' he said. 'Belial never saw it coming.'

Michael nodded in approval.

'There's no point getting old...' said Jonathan.

'If you don't get crafty,' said Michael, finishing Gabriel's favourite maxim. 'And I'm sorry about your father, Jonathan. I liked him.'

Jonathan turned to Savantha. 'But I have Mum.'

'That you do,' said Michael. 'So, what's your next adventure? Building dens in the forest, flying kites, chasing demon cats,' he pointed at Elgar where he sat on the windowsill.

'Well,' said Jonathan. 'Once Sam has shifted the portal back to Heaven, I'm going to fetch the book of creation from Uriel's tomb, and give it to Lucifer so he can stop the universe from coming apart like an old carpet.'

Michael coughed so hard that his face went purple. For a moment Jonathan thought the angel was having another episode.

'You're fetching *that* thing and giving it to Lucifer? Have we really got to the point of using the nuclear option?'

'Looks like it,' said Jonathan. 'You should see the size of the creature we cut in half outside Lucifer's castle. It all got a bit messy.'

Michael lay back on his pillows and puffed out his cheeks. 'What a strange state of affairs. I remember Gabriel locking that book up specifically to stop Lucifer or one of the Archdemons getting their hands on it. Now here we are going to fetch it for him. You haven't got any wine, have you? I really need a drink.'

'You are *not* having any wine,' Sammael called from downstairs.

Michael crossed his arms and scowled. 'Spoilsport.'

'Do you remember having a nightmare or something the other night?' asked Cay. 'You gave us a real scare. It was just before Lucifer appeared and told us it was all going nuts outside his castle. You were shouting about threads being cut and that something was very sharp.'

'Hmm,' said Michael, rubbing his forehead in concentration. 'I don't remember that. Maybe I just sensed that big rip appearing in Hell?'

Jonathan nodded, but now Cay had reminded him of Michael's outburst he felt uneasy; he just couldn't shake the feeling that something didn't add up.

'Penny for them?' asked Michael.

'Oh, it's nothing,' said Jonathan. 'I'm just tired.'

'Well,' said the angel. 'Why don't you sit here and tell me tales of your derring-do for a bit. Cay mentioned something about Lucifer turning Belial into furniture. That sounds hilarious, let's hear all about that.'

Jonathan couldn't help but smile at the angel, and so he described his battle with Belial and the Archdemon's particularly sticky end. But even as he told his tale, at the back of his mind he mulled over what Lucifer had asked him to do. Was handing over an artefact that could re-write the universe a good idea? If Jonathan was honest with himself, he really didn't know.

Chapter 12

Heaven Sent

Having had some breakfast and a brief nap, a weary Sammael limped upstairs to check on Michael. She found him awake and staring out of the window.

'You OK?' she asked.

'Sort of,' he replied. 'So much has changed while I… slept. It's quite a lot to take in and I'm still hungry. I could eat a horse, a very big horse.'

Sammael smiled. 'I'll have to ask Savantha to do some shopping for us. Elgar ate the last of the custard creams.'

'I was wondering what happened to my spear,' said Michael. 'Not having it by my side feels like losing an arm. Jonathan said he could help you make me another one when he's figured out how.'

'That's a possibility,' said Sammael. 'He's come a long way in a very short time. It'll take a while for him to fully understand Gabriel's gift.'

Michael nodded. 'Are you sure that fetching the book of creation from Uriel's tomb is the right thing to do?'

She looked out of the window, watching the weak winter sun sparkle on the snow-covered village. 'Yes,' she said. 'I've seen what waits for us unless we heal creation. This is the only way we can do it that doesn't involve a constant firefight. Lucifer may be a prideful, self-absorbed narcissist, but he hates the idea of anything he helped build being destroyed. I don't think he means any harm.'

Michael scratched the side of his nose and pondered. 'Well, if you say so. Have we seen or heard anything from Lilith? I guess having the other two Archdemons meet suitably unpleasant ends means she's decided to keep her head down and play nice.'

'One can but hope,' said Sammael. 'The last thing we need right now is her causing trouble. Right, I need to shift that portal; Jonathan has a job to do.'

'I'll come and watch,' said Michael. 'I think I might be able to make it to the front door without fainting. Being almost dead for such a long time does drain one so.' He grinned.

'Just don't push yourself,' said Sammael, kissing him on the forehead. 'Love you, little brother.'

'Oh, stop it,' said Michael, but he gave her hand a squeeze anyway.

Sammael left the room, and Michael swung his legs out of bed and reached for a dressing gown draped over the back of a chair. As he did so, a hairy, long-legged spider scurried out of the folds and aimed itself for a crack in the wall. It wasn't fast enough to evade being flattened by Michael's mallet-like fist. 'God, I hate spiders,' he said with a shudder, wiping his hand on the floor.

'I'm coming and that's final!' said Elgar.

'Me too,' said Cay. 'For once we're joining you. Mum and Dad said it's OK. We're going to explore Heaven, not some monster-infested bit of Hell.'

Jonathan sighed. 'Fine, but please don't... um... just don't... OK?'

'Have you any idea what he's burbling about?' Elgar asked Cay.

'I think he's asking us to avoid getting into trouble,' she replied.

'Pfft! Like we ever do that,' said the cat.

Jonathan rolled his eyes.

'So you have company?' said Sammael as she walked up.

'Apparently so,' said Jonathan.

'Well, let's get cracking then.' The angel steadied herself, and once again used her wing ribbons to move the portal from Lucifer's lands to the plaza outside Heaven. By the time she'd finished, sweat was pouring down her face and she could barely stand.

'Please rest, won't you?' Jonathan begged her.

'I don't have a choice,' groaned Sammael. 'I feel like a bag of spanners.'

'Good luck,' called a voice from the windmill. They all turned to see Michael waving at them from the doorway. He was dressed in a rather fetching floral-pattern dressing gown that was far too small for him.

'Nice dress,' Elgar called back.

Michael scowled.

'Behave,' said Jonathan, but he couldn't resist a smile. 'Right, let's go. Hopefully we won't be long.'

'Don't take any risks,' said Sammael. 'Let's hope you can actually open the door to Uriel's tomb. Given that Gabriel's blood runs in your veins you should be able to get in. You've got my directions?'

'Yep,' said Jonathan.

'I'll have the kettle on for when you get back. Be safe.'

Jonathan nodded and, accompanied by Elgar and Cay, he made his way through the portal and towards the gates of Heaven.

'I'm going to be the first demon cat to tread the hallowed halls,' purred Elgar. 'Happy days.'

'And I'm going to be the first werewolf,' said Cay, equally excited.

'You may be in for a shock,' said Jonathan, remembering his first glimpse of the devastation that Baal had wrought. The gates were open, and Jonathan couldn't resist running the tips of his fingers along the glass; it sang under his touch.

Just inside the gates a pair of angels stood to attention, fully armoured and with spears in their hands. They raised their eyebrows at the visitors but did nothing to stop them.

'Morning!' said Elgar. 'Lovely day for it.'

The angels had difficulty keeping a straight face.

'Oh my,' said Cay, as she looked around her.

'Yeah,' said Jonathan. 'Do you see what I mean now?'

Cay nodded. Above them was a blue sky and a bright sun, but its rays shone down on a scene of devastation. The remains of those who'd died had been collected and laid to rest with great reverence, but the damage caused by Baal was still very evident. Ruined buildings lay on all sides and stillness permeated the city.

'What must this have been like before?' asked Cay, her mouth wide open.

'It was... astonishing,' said Jonathan, seeing the place through Gabriel's eyes as they walked along the marble-paved boulevard. All around them, angels – their wings folded neatly against their backs – were gently and efficiently rebuilding their home. Jonathan knew it would take many years, but Heaven would recover. He had to remind himself that it was Lucifer who had saved so many of the angels, hiding them in his castle while Baal caused havoc.

They reached the great, ruined tree at the centre of Heaven. 'This is where you found Raphael, isn't it?' said Cay.

'He suffered so much,' said Jonathan. 'Out of all the

Archangels he had the worst of it. He lost his wife, his home, his family, and in the end Baal made sure he lost his mind. It's no wonder Sammael punished Baal in the way she did.'

'What's that up there?' asked Elgar.

Shielding his eyes against the sun, Jonathan peered through the bare and blackened branches. Right at the top of the tree was something that made his heart give a little squeeze inside his chest. It was a cluster of white blossom with a base of new green leaves. The tree wasn't dead after all, and that single fact made him incredibly happy.

'Life always finds a way,' said Elgar sagely.

'Certainly looks like it,' said Jonathan. 'C'mon, Uriel's tomb is this way.'

They marched past the tower where he'd found Michael, and entered a part of Heaven that Jonathan hadn't seen before. The devastation here was worse, and he wondered if the tomb was still intact.

'Have you any idea what we're going to find?' asked Elgar.

'Nope,' said Jonathan. 'I had a rummage through the library in my head while Sam was resting, but I couldn't find anything. It's as if Grandfather wiped his own memories of the place.'

'Why would he do that?' asked Cay.

'He would have had a reason,' said Jonathan. 'Gabriel never did anything randomly, but why is anyone's guess.'

'Well, let's hope we can get the door open,' said Elgar, 'or we're going to look really stupid.'

Another twenty minutes of walking brought them to an area that was patently a cemetery. Buildings gave way to memorials, mausoleums, and what would have been grass had the earth not been scorched to ash. 'I think this is the place,' said Jonathan. They walked in and, right at the back, built into the very wall that surrounded Heaven, was a door.

'Bingo,' said Jonathan.

'Doesn't look very impressive,' said Elgar.

'It doesn't need to be,' said Jonathan. 'This is the resting place of Uriel, last of the *Araelim*, the first angels to be created after Lucifer. He doesn't need anything to glorify his name.'

'You sound funny,' said Cay

Jonathan paused, then realised he'd been speaking the way Gabriel would have. He shook his head. 'Right, let's see if we can get in.' He touched the door with his hand. What he'd thought was blackened wood was actually dark glass; it felt warm under his fingers.

'Where's the handle?' asked Elgar.

'There doesn't appear to be one,' said Jonathan.

'And so it starts,' said Elgar. 'If Gabriel was here I'd bite him on the bum.'

Jonathan couldn't help but smile at the cat's irreverence.

He was right, Gabriel never made things easy, but given what the tomb contained that was hardly a surprise.

Just as he had when he'd spotted the secret door in Raphael's tower, Jonathan shut his eyes and extended his senses into the glass itself. The lock was actually quite simple, although as Sammael had said it was designed to respond only to Gabriel or members of his family. Taking a deep breath Jonathan asked it to open, and without hesitation the mechanism responded to his command. With a quiet click the glass door swung aside to reveal a flight of stone stairs leading downward.

'That was easy,' said Elgar. 'I take it all back.'

'Too easy?' suggested Cay.

'Let's find out, shall we?' said Jonathan, stepping through the door and walking down the steps. Elgar and Cay followed him, their way lit by panels in the ceiling that sprang into white luminescence as they passed. They reached a small landing, and found an ornate set of double doors set into a stone wall, rimmed with a thin strip of blue light. Above them was carved the name URIEL.

'This isn't just a door,' said Jonathan. 'Look at the light that surrounds it. It's a gate to somewhere else, just like the one in Gabriel's attic back in Hobbes End.'

'What, one of his pocket universes like where we found Brass?' asked Elgar.

'Maybe,' said Jonathan. 'Shall we have a look?'

Elgar and Cay both nodded.

This door had a handle, and trying not to show how nervous he felt, Jonathan turned it and pushed. The door swung open, and behind it was something they hadn't been expecting.

'I told you it was too easy,' said Elgar.

'You're not wrong,' said Jonathan.

Before them, stretching to the horizon in all directions, was a vast labyrinth. There were no walls, just stone paths with sheer drops on every side. 'I wonder how far down it goes?' said Elgar.

'Let's find out,' said Jonathan, fishing in his pocket. His fingers closed around a ten-pence piece and, extending his arm, he dropped the coin over the edge of the path. It fell, and they waited in silence for any noise that would indicate it had struck the ground. There was nothing.

'Well, at least we know not to step off the...' said Elgar, only to be interrupted as – with a whistle of air – the coin plummeted from above and dropped once again into the abyss.

'So... there really is no bottom to it,' said Cay. 'If you fall, you fall forever.'

'Great,' said Jonathan. 'Best we don't do that then.'

'What about some aerial reconnaissance?' said Elgar. 'That'd be a big help.'

'I'll give it a shot,' said Jonathan. 'I think I might have

the hang of it after yesterday. Let's hope I don't end up like that coin.'

'O ye of little faith,' said Elgar. 'Go on, faint heart never won fair lady, and all that guff.'

'OK,' said Jonathan, willing his wings to appear.

'And...?' said Elgar, as the seconds ticked by.

'That's odd,' said Jonathan. 'Hang on, let me try again.' Closing his eyes, he gathered his thoughts and visualised purple ribbons springing from his shoulders. Nothing happened.

'My wings have gone,' he gasped.

'What do you mean gone?' said Elgar. 'They can't just not be there.'

'Well, they're not,' said Jonathan, panic welling up inside him. 'I can't fly!'

Chapter 13

Tomb Raiding

'Well, that's just made my day,' said Elgar. 'To think I turned down a plate of custard creams for this.'

'That's not very helpful, is it?' said Jonathan, not sure whether to be annoyed or scared.

'But nothing's happened,' said Cay. 'All we did was walk in here.'

'I bet that's it,' said Jonathan, realisation dampening the awful thought that he'd lost all his powers. 'It's this place. Gabriel built this little world to keep Uriel's tomb safe, yeah?'

'Agreed,' said Elgar.

'Well, given how powerful Heaven's enemies were at the time, Gabriel would have designed it to account for that, sort of level the playing field.'

'Oh...' said Cay. 'I get it. It doesn't matter who or what you are, in here, you're just sort of...'

'Human?' said Elgar. 'Great, what's the point in having powers if you're not allowed to use them?'

'To stop you from stealing the most dangerous object in the universe?' suggested Cay.

'Oh yeah,' said Elgar. 'There is that.'

'This is deliberate,' said Jonathan, nodding as he thought it through. 'It's part of Gabriel's security measures.' Taking a deep breath he closed his eyes again. He may not have had his wings but he was still Gabriel's grandson. He could still think and he could still feel. Extending his senses, he tried to look at how his grandfather had put this place together. The picture was fuzzy, as if it didn't want to be seen, but Jonathan got what he needed to know. The mathematics used in the construction of the labyrinth were different from anything he'd seen before. They'd been altered somehow, shaped into something that didn't exude power, but rather drained it away to fuel itself. It didn't matter if Lucifer himself walked in here, there'd be no short cuts to Uriel's tomb, no flying, no opening gates, no nothing.

'What are we going to do?' asked Cay.

'We can't just go back empty-handed,' said Jonathan. 'There must be a way through the labyrinth; it's just a question of figuring out what it is.'

Elgar sniffed loudly.

'I know that sound,' said Cay. 'You smell something funny, don't you?'

'Not funny,' said Elgar. 'Not funny at all. There's something up ahead that smells of...'

'Of what?' asked Jonathan.

'Death,' said the cat.

Jonathan looked deeper into the maze, and in the distance, just where several paths intersected, he could see something dark and huddled on the white stone. 'What is that?' he said.

'Dunno,' said Elgar. 'But we might as well take a look. It doesn't appear to be moving.'

Jonathan looked at Cay and she shrugged. 'We might find something to help us?' she suggested.

Having thought of no other option they walked carefully onward, and as they drew nearer Jonathan could see why Elgar smelled death. The shape in front of them was not just some bundle of rags, it was the desiccated body of a male angel, his wings curled protectively round his knees where they were drawn up to his chest. On the ground next to him something had been written on the stone. The letters were crude and one of the angel's fingertips was resting just beneath them.

'He wrote something in his own blood,' gasped Cay. 'What does it say?'

Jonathan was about to run forward and find out when a hiss from Elgar stopped him.

'There's something wrong here,' said Elgar.

'Really, Sherlock? How'd you figure that one out?' said Cay.

Elgar ignored her sarcasm. 'No, I mean really wrong. This place may stop Jonathan from using his superpowers but it doesn't stop my nose. Everything smells off. What was Gabriel playing at?'

'What should we do?' Jonathan asked the cat.

'Stay here and let me do some sneaking,' said Elgar. 'I'm very good at it.'

'He's not wrong,' said Cay.

'Just be careful.'

Elgar nodded and slowly inched his way forward, belly touching the ground as though he was hunting. The cat reached the angel and peered at the writing on the stone. 'Oh dear,' he said.

'What does it say?' asked Jonathan.

'It says, Baal,' replied Elgar. 'How on earth did he manage to get an angel to..?' Elgar didn't have time to finish before the ground began to shake. A vast rumbling echoed all around, and without warning the paths in front of them started rearranging themselves into a completely different configuration.

'Oh hell!' cried Elgar, as the section of path he was sitting on suddenly swung sideways, taking both him and the dead angel away from the entrance to the tomb.

'Jump!' cried Jonathan and Cay in unison.

Not needing to be asked twice, the cat sprinted toward them and flung himself into space. He carved a graceful parabola through the air before catching the edge of the path at Jonathan's feet. With a look of horror, Elgar realised that, sharp though his claws were, they could find no purchase on the polished marble. Like a stone dropped down a well, he plummeted out of sight before anyone could grab him.

'NO!' screamed Jonathan as Elgar disappeared into the gloom.

'Hang on a minute,' said Cay.

'What?' said a distraught Jonathan.

'Look up. Remember the coin?'

He looked upward. There was no sign of the cat.

'Wait for it,' said Cay, grabbing hold of Jonathan's belt and leaning backwards. A high-pitched yowling grew louder as Elgar dropped towards them from above, and Jonathan readied himself to catch him. Just as the cat flashed past, Jonathan's hand shot out and grabbed on to whatever he could. He made contact with the furry tip of Elgar's tail and was yanked forward by the cat's momentum. If it hadn't been for Cay holding him back, he'd have gone over too.

'Got him!' shouted Jonathan.

'Got me?' shrieked Elgar as he dangled from Jonathan's hand. 'You almost dislocated my chuffing appendage!'

'Sorry,' said Jonathan slumping backward on to the path with Elgar in his lap.

'Oh the ignominy!' groaned the cat. 'I'm so glad Delius didn't see that. I'd never hear the end of it.'

All around them, the labyrinth continued to shift until it finally came to a stop in a totally different pattern from the one they'd seen when they came in. The body of the poor angel was nowhere in sight.

'This makes no sense,' said Jonathan.

'I agree,' said Elgar. 'What is your grandfather playing at? I didn't think he got his jollies from designing death-trap dungeons?'

'He didn't,' said Jonathan. 'He wouldn't.'

'This is impossible,' said Cay. 'We have a labyrinth so big we can't even see the far side, and that rearranges itself so you don't have a hope of finding your way to the middle, wherever that is? And where's Uriel's tomb?'

'I know,' said Jonathan. 'I don't understand why Grandfather would build something like this unless he was...'

'Unless he was what?' grumped Elgar, examining his tail for signs of damage.

'Unless he was... trying to make it impossible ever to get to the centre of the labyrinth, even for him.'

'Why would he do that?' asked Cay.

'Misdirection,' said Jonathan. 'He was being crafty, just like he always was.'

'Lost me,' said Elgar. 'Can I have the kitten version? My brain may have been damaged by my abrupt halt.'

'Look,' said Jonathan. 'Gabriel wanted to hide the book of creation, yeah?'

Elgar and Cay nodded.

'So he decided to send would-be thieves off on a wild

goose chase.' said Jonathan. 'This whole labyrinth is nothing more than a colossal waste of time. There is no way to the centre! The body of that angel: I bet when Baal had Raphael under his control, he got him to open the door and then send that angel down here to see if he could find the book. But there was no book to find. The poor guy must have starved to death looking for something that wasn't there.'

'But that's horrible,' said Cay

'Yeah, it is,' said Jonathan.

'If this whole thing is just a diversion, then where *is* Uriel's tomb?' asked Elgar.

'I bet it's right under our noses,' said Jonathan. 'Nobody knew what was down here except Gabriel, remember? Not Sam, not Michael and not Raphael. What better way to protect something so powerful than to hide it somewhere different from where everyone thinks it is.'

'Crafty old geezer,' said Elgar. 'So where's the book then?'

'Let's see,' said Jonathan. 'Follow me.' He walked back through the double doors. The second he was away from the influence of the labyrinth, he could feel his powers return and he sighed in relief. 'Right,' he said, peering at the walls, 'where are you?'

It was so cleverly blended with the stonework that Jonathan almost missed the secret door, similar to the one in Raphael's tower. No angelic power had been used in its construction, just basic mechanics. If you weren't looking for it you'd never know it was there.

'Hidden in plain sight,' he said.

'What is?' asked Cay.

'This,' said Jonathan, pressing on a section of the wall. There was an audible click and with a grinding sound a section swung inward to reveal a small chamber lit by the same luminescence that filled the corridor. In the centre of the chamber was a plain, stone sarcophagus.

'Uriel,' whispered Jonathan, 'the last of the *Araelim*.'

'Well, colour me impressed,' said Elgar. 'You really are starting to think like the old codger, aren't you?'

'I'll take that as a compliment,' said Jonathan.

'Shall we go in?' said Cay.

Jonathan nodded, and led the way to the sarcophagus. There was no lid, just a shimmering layer of white light, and beneath it lay the body of a male angel. He was dressed in formal robes, and his peaceful face was untouched by decay. His hands lay in his lap, fingers and thumbs pressed together as if he'd been holding something.

'The book of creation; it's gone!' said Jonathan.

'Do you think they'll be OK?' asked Michael, as he devoured his third sandwich of the morning.

'Yes,' said Sammael. 'Of course they will. All they have to do is enter the tomb and take the book from Uriel's hands.'

Michael raised his eyebrows. 'Our brother did have an odd sense of humour.'

'Gabriel wouldn't have left anything dangerous in the tomb... would he?' said Sammael.

'Nah,' said Michael. 'But then again, you never knew what was going on in that brain of his.'

'Fine, I'll go and see where they've got to,' said Sammael, groaning in pain as she levered herself out of her chair. She'd barely taken a step when Jonathan, Cay and Elgar walked into the windmill. She tried to read the looks on their faces but all she saw was confusion.

'Well?' she asked. 'Did you find it?'

'It depends what you mean by *found*,' said Elgar.

Sammael shook her head. 'What?'

'We located the tomb all right,' said Jonathan, 'after getting past Gabriel's security measures.'

'Told you,' said Michael with his mouth full.

'And?' asked Sammael. 'Was the book with Uriel's body?'

'I think it was, once,' said Jonathan.

'What he's trying to say,' said Elgar, 'is that someone got there before us. That book Lucifer wanted to use to fix creation? Someone's already nicked it!'

The only sound that could be heard following that announcement was a soft thud, as the remains of Michael's huge sandwich fell to the floor.

Chapter 14

Back to Square One

Sammael stared at Elgar, her eyes wide with shock. 'What do you mean *someone's nicked it!*'

'Just that,' said Elgar. 'Uriel's body was there, perfectly preserved, and his hands looked like they'd been holding something, but there was no book.'

'Sadly, he's right,' said Jonathan. 'You wouldn't believe the lengths Gabriel went to in securing that tomb. We found a dead angel that Baal had sent in to try and find the book; the poor guy starved to death and never made it out.'

'Will there ever be an end to the damage that monster caused?' said Sammael. 'Well, at least he didn't succeed. If he had we'd have known about it a long time ago. The question is who took the book of creation and where is it now?'

'I have absolutely no idea,' said Jonathan. 'I couldn't find anything about the book or the tomb in Gabriel's memories. It's like he deliberately wiped them clean.'

'Hmm, that sounds just like my big brother,' said

Michael, trying to recover the remains of his sandwich without getting too much fluff on it. 'We were at war at the time. He knew that if he was captured by Lucifer or the Archdemons they might torture the book's location out of him, so he made sure they couldn't, regardless of what they did.'

'That makes sense,' said Jonathan. 'But it doesn't help us. What are we going to tell Lucifer?'

'The truth,' said Sammael. 'I'll go and do it. Maybe I can stop him from throwing his toys out of the pram.'

For some reason that image made Jonathan smile; he couldn't imagine the fallen angel having a tantrum.

'I guess we're back to square one,' said Cay.

'It looks like it,' said Sammael. 'But I can't think of a way to save creation without the book. It's only a matter of time before everything starts to fall apart and we can't stop it. How did it come to this?'

Jonathan gave his great-aunt's hand a squeeze. He could see how troubled she was, and he didn't want her to start blaming herself again. 'We'll figure something out,' he said. 'The book must be out there somewhere; it's just a question of figuring out who took it.'

'I wish I shared your optimism,' she said. 'Right, where's my coat? I'm going to have to shift the portal again and go and see Lucifer in person, see if I can stop him losing it.'

'You're supposed to be resting,' said Jonathan.

'I know, but what choice do I have?' She gave him a sad smile. 'I caused this problem when I killed Baal and it's my responsibility to fix it, no matter the cost.'

'OK, but don't push yourself too hard.'

'I won't, don't worry. The sunlight will do me good.' She kissed him on the forehead and shuffled out of the windmill, the weight of the world on her shoulders.

'I wish I knew where the book of creation was,' said Jonathan, watching his great-aunt as she limped through the snow, trying to ignore the pain of her injuries.

'Don't fret about her, lad,' said Michael. 'She was always a worrier. Me, I just liked hitting stuff with my spear.'

'You'll get on very well with Grimm,' said Cay. 'He has the same feelings about his cricket bat!'

'Damn it!' said Lilith, thumping her hand against the rim of the scrying pool. 'How can it be gone? Belial didn't take it and neither did Baal. Where is it hiding, hmm?'

'You've got me,' said Flay, slowly rasping a whetstone along the blade of his skinning knife.

'Stop that!' barked Lilith. 'I'm trying to think.'

Flay snorted. 'What are you going to do?'

'There's not much I can do but wait,' said Lilith. 'They mustn't know of my involvement until I've got my hands on the book. If I make a move too soon they'll be on their guard, and I don't want to spoil the surprise. I'm looking forward to seeing the looks on their faces when they realise the truth. It'll make their destruction all the more amusing.'

'I agree,' said Flay. 'I haven't killed anything worthy in ages and it's boring me.'

'You'll get your chance,' said Lilith. 'I'll stay my wrath until they've figured out where the book is and then – and only then – do we strike.'

'It's funny,' said Flay, testing the edge of his razor-sharp blade against the ball of his thumb.

'What is?' said Lilith.

'They'll be running around like little ants, desperately trying to find the thing they think will save the universe, when in fact they're signing its death warrant. I love irony almost as much as assassination – it makes me happy.'

Jonathan, Cay and Elgar crunched their way across the village green. The sun was shining, and the snow and ice which covered everything sparkled like a carpet of diamonds; it was quite beautiful.

'I can't imagine losing all this,' he said, 'after everything that's happened, all the people who've died to save it. It's awful.'

'I know,' said Cay. 'Let's hope we can think of something before another of those monsters decides it wants in.'

They heard a snort from the pond and turned to see the tip of Brass' snout peeping above the surface. The rest of the dragon was submerged in the water which never froze.

'I don't think she likes the cold,' said Elgar. 'Until she came here she lived in a desert.'

'Well, at least she's happy with her new home,' said Jonathan. 'And we still need to find a suitable Christmas tree before Ignatius and Grimm get back from Devon.'

'Good luck persuading Brass to go and fetch it,' said Elgar. 'After the battering she took I don't think she wants to go ferreting around in the forest at the moment.'

They were almost at Cay's house when they saw the familiar, black-clad form of Mr Peters walking towards them.

'Good afternoon,' he said, smiling. 'Why the long faces?'

'You wouldn't believe the morning we've had,' said Elgar. 'My poor tail.'

Mr Peters looked confused.

'It's a long story,' said Cay. 'We're trying to find something important to save the universe and it's gone missing.'

'Ah,' nodded Mr Peters. 'It's always the case. I find that trying to think of the last place you saw it often helps.'

'Been there, done that,' said Elgar.

'In that case, try not thinking about it for a bit,' said Mr Peters. 'The answer often comes to you when you're doing something else. In fact, that was what I wanted to see you about. I've found something you may be interested in, Cay.'

'Oh really?' she said. 'What?'

'Well, it's a bit of a walk but I think you'll enjoy the surprise.'

'It doesn't involve being eaten by alien squid monsters does it?' asked Elgar.

'Um, no,' said Mr Peters. 'Why don't you follow me and find out.'

'OK,' said Cay. 'Let's go. You both coming?' she asked Jonathan and Elgar.

'Might as well,' said Jonathan. 'Maybe the walk will help me clear my head.'

Mr Peters smiled and led them past the churchyard and towards the forest, behind where Gabriel's cottage used to be. While Cay chatted to Mr Peters, Jonathan hung back and let the silence of the winter forest envelop him. The only noise was the soft crunch of snow under his boots, and the stillness went a great way towards calming his racing mind. He had so many unanswered questions, and once again had so little time in which to answer them. Not a day went by that he didn't wish Gabriel and his father were still here to help him learn, but they were gone, and he would have to make do with their memories to comfort him when he felt lost, just as he did right now.

'I wonder where we're going?' asked Elgar, bounding through the snow at Jonathan's side.

'I dunno. I don't really mind. Any distraction from the end of the universe would be nice.'

'I hear ya,' agreed the cat.

They trudged onward until they were deep in a part of the forest Jonathan hadn't been to before. The lake where Cay had first encountered Raven of the Corvidae was off to their right somewhere, and as there were no real paths through the trees they had to push their way through bushes and scrub.

'Are we there yet?' asked Elgar. 'My paws are freezing.'

'Almost,' said Mr Peters. 'Now, please be very quiet, I don't want you to scare them.'

'Scare who?' asked Cay.

'You'll see, now hush.'

They did as Mr Peters asked and followed him as quietly as they could. Before long they came to the edge of a small clearing. 'Sit here,' he said, gesturing to the ground behind the trunk of a fallen tree. 'We need to keep ourselves hidden.'

'Don't tell me we've actually got goblins or something living here,' said Elgar. 'That would be fun.'

'Oh, much better than that,' said Mr Peters, taking off his wide-brimmed hat. Jonathan saw how pale the old man was, but his hair was still surprisingly black, albeit with grey at the temples. Mr Peters sensed he was being studied and turned to look at Jonathan. 'Still think I'm a vampire?' he said, wiping sweat from his forehead with a white handkerchief.

'That was all Cay,' said Jonathan.

'So, I was wrong,' she said, shrugging her shoulders.

Mr Peters chuckled to himself. 'That's in the past. This however, is the present. Look at that pile of branches over there and wait.'

They did as they were told and sat quietly; the only sound in the forest around them was the soft *flumpf* of snow falling from tree branches.

Jonathan's feet started to go numb. He was about to shift position when he heard a soft yelp. He looked at Elgar.

'It wasn't me,' mouthed the cat.

Mr Peters pointed to the pile of branches. They all looked, and were rewarded with the extraordinary sight of a tiny wolf cub nosing its way out its den. Its fur was silver-white, and it seemed utterly perplexed by the concept of snow.

Cay stifled a gasp and grabbed hold of Mr Peters' arm. Her face was alight with happiness. The old man smiled at her. 'I thought you might like this,' he whispered.

Another cub followed, and then another, until there were three of them rolling and playing. They made soft yelping sounds as they nipped gently at each other, enjoying the rough and tumble and snorting when snow got up their noses.

Cay tried to get up, but Mr Peters put out a restraining hand and shook his head. The reason quickly became obvious. Following on the heels of the cubs, two adult wolves emerged from the den and joined the play-fighting. Soon the entire family was romping in the snow, unaware they were being watched.

'*Canis lupus*, the timber wolf,' Mr Peters whispered in Cay's ear. 'They've not been seen in the wild in England for over five hundred years. I think they must have escaped from a zoo or private collection and made their way to Hobbes End, as do all those who need a place to be safe. They are exquisite, are they not?'

Cay could only nod and gaze at the family at play, tears of joy in her eyes.

'Wow,' Elgar whispered to Jonathan. 'I've got to admit that's really something. Remind me not to come out this way on my own. I don't want to end up as a doggy treat.'

Much to the alarm of Mr Peters, Cay shook off his hand and stood up. The adult wolves froze and stared at her while the cubs carried on playing, oblivious to the new arrival.

'Cay!' hissed Jonathan. 'Get down.'

She shook her head, and carefully swung her legs over the fallen tree trunk until she was sitting on it. Without showing any fear at all she slowly extended her right hand. For a moment Jonathan wondered what was going to happen, and then, in astonishment, he watched as the mother wolf slowly padded across the clearing. She cautiously sniffed Cay's outstretched hand before licking it gently. 'Hello, beautiful one,' Cay said, stroking the she-wolf behind the ears. The wolf responded by arching her head back so Cay could tickle her under the chin.

'Well,' whispered Mr Peters. 'There's something you don't see every day.'

The male wolf joined his mate, and together they let Cay stroke them without any sign of fear or aggression. Jonathan marvelled at the way they seemed completely at ease with her, no doubt sensing she was as much a wolf as she was a girl. It was a sight that would stay with him for the rest of his life.

'I've never seen an ordinary wolf,' said Elgar. 'They don't act like they do in the stories, all huffing and puffing and blowing your house down.'

'No,' said Jonathan, 'they certainly...' his voice trailed off as a distant memory surfaced from deep inside him; a memory of being very young, of his father, of being read fairy tales, and of a book with a lock on it that he hadn't been allowed to touch. For a moment he could do nothing but sit and stare as puzzle pieces fell together in his head. With his heart pounding he turned to look at Elgar.

'You OK?' whispered the cat. 'You look like you've seen a ghost.'

'I have, sort of,' said Jonathan. 'I might be completely wrong, but I think I know who took the book from Uriel's tomb and where it is now!'

Chapter 15

Blast from the Past

Jonathan forced himself to keep calm as Cay finished greeting the wolves, and watched as they trotted away and back to their young, nudging them towards the den with their noses. With a last flash of silver fur they were gone and the clearing was empty once more.

'I come and watch them every day,' said Mr Peters. 'They had their pups late this year, maybe they wanted to reach the safety of this forest before bringing them into this world?'

'Aren't they scared of you?' asked Cay.

'No,' said Mr Peters. 'I've always liked wolves. The forests of my homeland were full of them, and when I was young I used to sit and watch them for hours. They seemed to know I was not a threat. And now, well, I'm just an old man with sensitive skin.'

'Where was your homeland?' asked Cay.

'A long way away from here,' he replied. 'I'll tell you about it one day, but it's getting dark and we need to get back.'

Cay nodded. 'Thank you, Vladimir,' she said.

The old man smiled and got stiffly to his feet. 'And did the two of you enjoy such a rare sight?' he asked Jonathan and Elgar. They both nodded, and Cay saw that Jonathan had a familiar look on his face, the one that said he'd had an idea and wanted to find out if he was right.

They followed their trail back through the forest, and as they walked Cay couldn't restrain her curiosity. 'You've had one of your thoughts, haven't you?'

'I have lots of thoughts,' said Jonathan, grinning at her.

'You know what I mean,' said Cay, giving him a shove that almost sent him headfirst into a snowdrift.

'It was something Elgar said about wolves in stories,' said Jonathan. 'I remembered my dad reading to me when I was little, and that he had this old book on a shelf in his study that I wasn't allowed to touch. He said it was a first edition of Grimm's fairy tales and that it was very valuable; it even had this little lock on it to keep the pages shut.'

'Well, I wouldn't want a four-year-old getting jammy fingerprints on something like that either,' said Cay.

'Maybe,' said Jonathan. 'But it got me thinking. We moved house a lot, and I remember looking for the book when I was a bit older but I couldn't find it. I'd forgotten about it until now.'

'And you think this book of fairy stories has something to do with the book of creation?'

'Maybe,' said Jonathan. 'We've got no other leads.'

'But how would it end up with your dad?'

'I think Gabriel took it with him when he left Heaven,' said Jonathan. 'That gap in his memories is bugging me. Look, I just need to get to the vicarage and check something, then we'll see if I'm right.'

'Fair enough,' said Cay. 'A cup of hot chocolate and some detective work sounds like a good way to spend a winter's evening!'

By the time they got back to Hobbes End, darkness had fallen and they were all frozen solid. After thanking Mr Peters for showing them such a lovely sight, they made their way to the vicarage.

'Evening,' said Montgomery, as they walked up.

'Hi,' said Jonathan. 'Everything OK?'

'Yep,' said Stubbs. 'Nowt to report. Where've you been?'

'We went to see a family of timber wolves that have moved into the forest,' said Cay. 'They had cubs!'

'Ahh,' said Stubbs. 'Cute. Can we come and see them too?'

'Sure,' said Jonathan. 'Mr Peters said he goes there every day. I'm sure he'd take you along if you ask him.'

'Cool,' nodded Montgomery, piled-up snow falling off his head. 'We'll go tomorrow.'

'Can we go inside, please?' groaned Elgar. 'I can't feel my paws and my tail is throbbing.'

'Yeah, let's go,' said Jonathan. 'See you in the morning, guys.'

The gargoyles grinned, and settled into a heated discussion about what names they could give the cubs.

'You do know that Stubbs is going to want to call one of them Susan, don't you?' said Elgar as they reached the front door. 'He cracks me up.'

Once inside they hung up their coats, pulled off their boots and walked into the kitchen where Savantha sat reading the paper.

'You all look frozen,' she said. 'Let's get you a hot drink, shall we?'

While Jonathan and Cay sat down and rubbed their feet to bring back the circulation, Elgar hopped into the sink, put in the plug and turned on the hot tap.

'Another bath?' asked Savantha.

'Yep,' said the cat, smiling in happiness as the water covered his paws and tail. 'It's been a trying day.'

'I wonder how Ignatius and Grimm are doing?' said Jonathan, once he had a mug of hot chocolate in his hands.

'They called earlier,' said Savantha. 'I filled them in on developments and managed to stop them from coming home early. They'll be back tomorrow evening as originally scheduled.'

Jonathan nodded, happy that his friends hadn't needed to race back to help with yet another crisis. 'Right,' he said, 'time to have a look in Ignatius' study.'

'What are you going in there for?' asked Savantha.

'I need to have a look in the journal of Augustus Crumb.'

'Why?'

'Because I want to see if my grandfather was the one who stole the book of creation.'

Savantha coughed and spluttered as a mouthful of tea went down the wrong way. 'Why would Gabriel take it?' she asked. 'He was the one who locked it away in the first place.'

'He did,' said Jonathan. 'Back then he wanted to make sure it was safe from Lucifer and the Archdemons. But things changed, didn't they? All because Baal sneaked into Heaven and drove Raphael insane. When Grandfather exiled himself there was no way he was going to leave that book behind. He knew something was wrong with Raphael and couldn't risk him doing something stupid. Raphael was his brother and he could open the door to Uriel's tomb just as easily as Gabriel. He might not have found the book given the labyrinth diversion, but that was a risk Grandfather couldn't take, so he stole the book himself.'

Savantha smiled at her son. 'You sound more and more like him, you know.'

'Part of his *gift*, I guess,' said Jonathan. 'And there's something else. Gabriel erased anything to do with the book from the knowledge he gave me, there's nothing there. Why would he do that unless he wanted to hide something? He didn't want anyone to know what he'd done, even me. All he wanted was to keep that book safe.'

'It's a good theory,' said Elgar, sitting on the draining board and rubbing himself down with a tea towel. 'How do we prove it?'

'The journal of Augustus Crumb,' said Jonathan. 'He was vicar when Gabriel crash landed here. Maybe he saw something and wrote it down? Look, this could just be a wild goose chase but it makes sense, yeah?'

'Nobody else has come up with anything,' said Cay. 'Let's go and see.'

Mugs in hand, they wandered through to Ignatius' study. Jonathan felt odd going inside when the vicar wasn't there. It was his private space and it felt like he was intruding somehow. Savantha brushed some dust from the framed photograph of Ignatius' wife and son that sat on his roll-top desk.

'He's an amazing man,' she said. 'Despite all he's suffered he never gave up on this village, or himself.' She looked at Jonathan, her eyes bright with unshed tears. 'If I'd lost you as well as Darriel I don't know what I'd have done.'

'But you didn't,' said Jonathan, giving her a hug.

'Enough of the mushy stuff,' said Elgar, jumping onto the desk and rolling his eyes. 'Get the journal out of the bookcase and let's have a look.'

Jonathan flicked the cat's ear and did as Elgar asked. He

remembered looking through the journals when he'd first come to the village, back when they had been trying to figure out how Rook, Raven and Crow of the Corvidae were able to bypass Hobbes End's defences. On the top shelf, first in the row, was the old, leatherbound volume belonging to Augustus Crumb. Jonathan slid it out, sat himself at Ignatius' desk and carefully turned the brittle pages until he found the entry he was looking for; the one dated the second of September 1666.

The spidery writing was faded and some of the words were spelled oddly, but Jonathan managed to make sense of it. 'Listen to this,' he said, reading out loud.

'*Today I witnessed something that will stay with me until I breathe my last. With these very eyes I saw an angel fall from Heaven, and of all the places he could have touched this earth he chose this humble village. He was hurt, with great burns on his body, and I alone pulled him from the waters of the pond. I do not chide my flock for being too scared to help, but I knew I had to do something. I do not know how he can still be alive after such a journey, but he is resting here under my very roof and I think he will recover. I spoke to him, and he told me his name was Gabriel, at which juncture I had to take some wine to calm my own nerves. He seemed unconcerned about his injuries, but would not let the package he'd brought with him from Heaven out of his sight. When I asked what it was he smiled at me and said that there are some things one cannot bear to leave behind, however far from home one travels. He sleeps now, but I cannot. This is truly a time of wonders, and I want to watch the dawn rise on a new day for us all.'*

'Oh...' said Elgar. 'Care to guess what Gabe couldn't leave behind?'

'I think your theory may be right, Jonathan,' said Savantha, leaning over her son's shoulder. 'Is there anything else?'

'No,' he said. 'The next few entries are all about trying to persuade the villagers that it wasn't the end of the world.'

'Well, since you're playing at consulting detective, if Gabriel did bring the book with him, where do you think he hid it?' asked Savantha.

Jonathan looked at Cay and she grinned back at him. 'I think he gave it to Dad,' he said.

Savantha blinked. 'What?'

'I think he gave it to Dad.'

'But... but...' Savantha burbled.

'It was something Elgar said when we were watching the wolves in the forest,' said Jonathan.

'Wolves?'

'Oh yeah,' said Cay. 'A family of timber wolves have moved in.'

'Just like Augustus, I need a drink,' said Savantha. 'I wonder if Grimm has any wine stashed in the pantry along with the tea?'

'I remembered that Dad would read to me before bed when I was little,' said Jonathan. 'But there was this one book he would never let me touch. It was big and it had a lock on it. He said it was a first edition of Grimm's fairy tales and that I mustn't play with it.'

Savantha smiled. 'I remember that,' she said. 'We were travelling in Germany and he found it in a bookshop. It was very expensive and he didn't want to buy it, but I went back later and bought it myself without him knowing. I gave it to him as a present on our next anniversary. It was very special to both of us, but I don't think it's the book you're looking for, Jonathan. I'm sorry.'

'Oh,' he said, utterly crestfallen.

'It was a good idea though,' said Savantha. 'If Gabriel did bring the book from Heaven then he obviously hid it somewhere, but it's not that book of fairy tales. Sleep on it, you've all had a long day and I really do need a glass of wine.' Giving Jonathan's shoulder a squeeze, she went to rummage in the pantry.

'That's annoying,' said Elgar. 'I got all excited for a minute.'

Jonathan thumped the desk. 'I was so sure!'

'I know,' said Cay. 'I'm sorry. I should get home before Mum and Dad send out a search party. You know how twitchy they get.'

Jonathan nodded.

'See ya in the morning.'

'What have I missed, Elgar?' said Jonathan.

When he didn't receive a reply he turned round to find the cat chomping on something. Wildly flailing spindly legs protruded from Elgar's lips as the cat stared at him.

'What is it with cats and spiders?' said Jonathan. 'Please just eat it rather than spitting out some half-chewed mess on the carpet!'

Chapter 16

Riding in Cars with Gargoyles

Jonathan awoke early. He'd been tossing and turning for hours and finally decided that enough was enough. Pulling on his dressing gown, he drew the curtains and perched himself on the windowsill. The village was still in darkness, although lights plinked on here and there as the inhabitants of Hobbes End began their day.

His failure to figure out where the book was hidden gnawed at him. He knew deep down that Gabriel had brought it with him from Heaven; he could feel it in his blood despite the angel's attempts to erase all memory of it. The question was where had his grandfather hidden it? Jonathan had pondered this conundrum all night and was determined to chase down every lead regardless of how slim it might be.

His mother had said that the book of fairy tales wasn't what they were looking for, but there was something that kept bringing his mind back to it again and again. Darriel had always involved Jonathan in everything he did, and that book was the only thing he could remember his father not letting him touch.

He thought about what Savantha had said the previous night, and Jonathan grinned as an adventure brewed in his mind, a cunning plan that might just kill two birds with one stone. Christmas was only a few days away and, up until now, he hadn't known what to give his mother as a present. After a year of such cataclysmic change he wanted to give her something that showed just how much he loved her, and now he knew what; the trick was fetching it without her knowing.

'I need to be crafty, Grandfather, don't I?' he whispered, his breath frosting on the glass. He heard his mother pottering around downstairs, so he decided to get dressed and put his plan into action.

'You're up early,' said Savantha, as Jonathan walked into the kitchen.

'Yeah, I didn't sleep very well. What are you up to today?'

'I'm going into town in a bit. There are still a few things I need to get for Christmas and I want to beat the crowds. I don't want Grimm having to rush out the moment he gets back because he's missing a tin of biscuits or something. You know how pernickety he is about the contents of the pantry.'

Jonathan nodded, hiding his excitement at his mother's imminent absence. This was perfect timing.

'What are your plans?' she asked.

'I thought I'd have a closer look at what's left of Gabriel's cottage,' he lied, shamelessly. 'Maybe there's some clue in the rubble that might help?'

'Good idea. You can fill me in when I get back. I shouldn't be too long, mid-afternoon hopefully. Right, I'm off. Get yourself some breakfast and be good.' She kissed him on the forehead and trudged out to her car.

Jonathan was pondering how to get transport of his own when the cat flap banged open and Elgar sauntered in. 'Morning,' he said, puffing snow from his whiskers. It took him a whole two seconds to figure out that something was up. 'You've been scheming,' he said to Jonathan. 'You've got that look on your face again; it's the one that says you're about to do something that's way outside what a responsible adult would deem to be acceptable. I'm in, whatever it is.'

Jonathan grinned. 'We're going on a road trip,' he said. 'I just need to speak to the gargoyles and see if they want to help.'

'And where are we going?' asked Elgar.

'To my parents' old cottage.'

'What, the one that got destroyed when the Corvidae first attacked you?'

Jonathan nodded.

'You've really got a bee in your bonnet about this book of fairy tales, haven't you?' said the cat.

'It's for Mum,' said Jonathan. 'She gave it to Dad for their anniversary, and I want to see if I can find it and give it back to her for Christmas.'

'Ahh,' said Elgar. 'Sweet. I take it Cay will be coming?'

'Like I could stop her,' said Jonathan. 'C'mon, let's get cracking.'

Pulling on his coat and boots, Jonathan left the vicarage with Elgar at his side, unaware that eight glittering eyes were watching him from above the kitchen door.

The gargoyles were still half-asleep and Jonathan had to throw snowballs at them to wake them up.

'Oh, come on!' moaned Stubbs. 'It's way too early.'

'I agree with my learned friend,' said Montgomery with a huge yawn.

'I need your help,' said Jonathan. 'Top-secret mission and stuff.'

'We're in,' said Stubbs. 'I'm sick of sitting here freezing my granite butt off.'

'Do you actually feel the cold?' asked Elgar.

'Well, no, not really,' said Stubbs. 'But it's the principle of the thing.'

'Do you remember that conversation we had over the summer when you mentioned you'd driven Salvador Crumb's car?' asked Jonathan.

'Oh yeah,' said Stubbs. 'Monty was in charge of the steering wheel and gearstick and I did the pedals. Right laugh that was until we crashed it. Salvador had a sense of humour failure after that.'

'It was a bit of a banger, though,' said Montgomery. 'I always wanted to be a racing driver. I'd love to have a go with Grimm's Daimler but he'd probably cement me to the gatepost if I tried.'

'Just what I wanted to hear,' said Jonathan. 'Do you fancy being chauffeurs today?'

'Do we ever,' said Stubbs, hopping up and down with excitement.

'I gotta fetch something before we go,' said Montgomery. 'Where should we meet you?'

'Mr Peters' house.'

'Genius. See you there in a mo.'

The gargoyles scurried into the vicarage while Jonathan and Elgar crossed the green. They knocked at the door to one of the cottages and a fully dressed Mr Peters opened it.

'Good morning,' he said. 'To what do I owe such an early visit?'

'Do you ever sleep?' asked Elgar.

'Not much. It's part of being very old. You tend to want to use all the time you have left profitably.'

'I've got a favour to ask,' said Jonathan.

Mr Peters nodded.

'Mum wants to go into town but her car's got a flat battery. Can she borrow yours, please?'

Mr Peters looked at him for a moment as if weighing up something inside his head. The corner of his mouth twitched with the beginning of a smile. 'Oh, I see. Well, we can't have that, can we?' He fished in his pocket for his car keys and handed them to Jonathan. 'I was just on my way to watch the wolves again so I won't be back for a while.'

'You saw Mum leave, didn't you?' said Jonathan.

'Ah, these old eyes of mine are not what they once were,' replied Mr Peters, stepping into the snow and shutting the door behind him. 'Please tell your... mum... to be careful. The roads are slippery and finding second gear in my car is tricky. Have a good day.'

He touched the brim of his hat, smiled, and walked off towards the forest.

'Kerching!' said Elgar.

'Right, let's grab Cay and get out of here before we're seen,' said Jonathan.

They jogged round to the village shop. Cay was already peering out of her bedroom window. Not wanting to alert Mr and Mrs Forrester, Jonathan beckoned her to come down. She gave him the thumbs up, and a couple of minutes later appeared at the front door.

'What's going on?' she asked.

'No time to explain,' said Jonathan, 'just come with us.'

Grabbing her coat, Cay did as she was told and followed him to the lean-to where Mr Peters kept his car, an old Volkswagen Beetle. Standing next to it were the gargoyles.

'What on earth are you wearing?' Elgar asked Montgomery.

'My driving gear,' he said happily.

Jonathan and Cay couldn't stop giggling at the sight of the little gargoyle wearing goggles and driving gloves that were far too large for him.

'It's not 1936, Monty,' said Elgar. 'Cars have lids and windscreens now.'

'The gargoyle put his hands on his hips and scowled. 'It's the...'

'Yeah, yeah, I know,' said Elgar, 'it's the principle of the thing.'

'Exactly,' said Montgomery. 'Keys please.'

Jonathan handed them over, and the gargoyle climbed into the driver's seat while Stubbs ensconced himself in the footwell. 'Remind me which pedal is the clutch?' he asked.

Elgar looked at Jonathan. 'If this all goes horribly wrong I was asleep in my basket the whole time, understand?'

'What is happening?' asked Cay.

'We're going for a drive,' said Jonathan.

'But where? Does your mum know?'

'To the cottage where I used to live and no, she doesn't, and it's going to stay that way.'

'Oh,' said Cay. 'Then I guess I'm in the back with the cat. It's about time someone else apart from me did something daft.'

Happy that Cay didn't seem to mind the concept of a thoroughly illegal drive in the snow, Jonathan jumped into the passenger seat. 'Off we go then. Belt up everyone,' he said. 'I'll navigate.'

'Tally ho!' said Monty, turning the key in the ignition.

The engine spluttered into life, and with some weirdly accurate teamwork from the gargoyles, they pulled out of the drive and chugged slowly round the edge of the green.

'Does Sam know what you're doing?' asked Cay.

'Nope,' said Jonathan, his eyes fixed on the road ahead.

'That's a shame, because she's standing by the vicarage with her hands on her hips and I don't think she approves.'

Jonathan glanced to his right. His great-aunt was indeed standing outside the vicarage, a quite extraordinary look on her face. As they drew level, Montgomery wound the window down and waved at her. 'Riding in cars with gargoyles!' he called out, a manic grin on his face.

'Won't be long,' added Jonathan.

Sammael watched open-mouthed as the Beetle gathered speed and, spraying snow from its back wheels, shot towards the forest road and out of Hobbes End. She stood there for a good minute after the car had disappeared, wondering whether she should go after them. Heaving a sigh and with the cold making her injuries throb, she decided that just for today she simply couldn't be bothered to make a fuss. Flicking snow from her face, she went back to her windmill where she hoped Michael had left her some bacon and eggs.

'The wheels on the bus go round and round,' sang Montgomery.

'Round and round,' echoed Stubbs from the footwell.

The car bumped and rattled along until it came to the boundary of Hobbes End, a long hawthorn hedge with a red postbox peeping out of it.

'Where to, guv'?' asked Montgomery.

'Take a left,' said Jonathan. Then keep going for two miles before taking a right.'

'Righto. Mr Stubbs, if you please?'

'Consider it done, Mr Montgomery,' replied Stubbs, pressing the throttle as hard as he could. The little car leapt forward, and with wipers flip-flopping flakes of snow from the windscreen, Jonathan turned to Cay.

'You're going after that old book of fairy stories, aren't you?' she said.

Jonathan nodded. 'Yeah. If I can find it I want to give it to Mum for Christmas, and I can't shake the feeling there's more to it. I was thinking about it all last night. If Gabriel stole the book of creation from Uriel's tomb, he would have been worried that Raphael would eventually find out. It wouldn't have taken much for Raphael to realise that only Gabriel could have taken it.'

'Yeah, that makes sense,' said Cay.

'So, if Gabriel wanted to keep the book *really* safe, he may have wanted to get it away from Hobbes End and leave it with someone he could trust.'

'Like your dad,' said Cay.

'Exactly,' said Jonathan.

'But your mum said that the book of fairy stories and the book of creation aren't the same thing.'

'I know,' said Jonathan. 'I can't explain it but I think the two are linked somehow. I just have to go and look. Our cottage was the last place I saw my dad alive.'

'I know,' said Cay. 'You haven't been back since, have you?'

'Not until today,' said Jonathan, 'but if Gabriel did give the book of creation to Dad for safekeeping it'll be there, and if it is I'm gonna find it!'

Chapter 17

Father to Son

The little car churned its way along country roads bordered with bare trees and empty fields. Mercifully there was little traffic, and the only occasion that gave Jonathan a fright was when they had to stop to let another car go past. The adults paid them no attention whatsoever, but the little girl in the back seat waved at Montgomery and smiled as she sailed by.

'How much farther?' asked Elgar. 'I get car sick, you know.'

'Just one more turning,' said Jonathan. 'There it is, just up ahead.'

'Got it,' said Montgomery, flipping the indicator.

'I must admit, you two aren't that bad at driving,' said Elgar. 'For gargoyles.'

'Thank you,' came Stubbs' muffled reply.

As they drove along the narrow lane Jonathan's heart beat faster. Beyond the next bend lay the place that he'd called home until three monsters in bowler hats changed his life for ever. He'd often thought of asking his mother if they could come back here but something always stopped him. He knew what it was: the memory of his father standing in the cellar and screaming at them to run before he brought the house down on top of them. And yet here Jonathan was, eight months later and with nothing but a hunch to guide him. It would be his first Christmas without his dad, and if he could find that book of fairy tales then he knew he could at least give his mother a present she would treasure. And maybe, just maybe, it would give him a clue to where Gabriel had hidden the book of creation.

They drew level with the entrance to the cottage and Montgomery parked the car expertly.

'Thanks, guys. Well driven,' said Jonathan.

'Our pleasure,' chorused the gargoyles.

'C'mon, everybody,' said Elgar. 'I want to see what all the fuss is about.'

They clambered out of the car, and Jonathan looked upon the remains of his home for the first time since he and his mother had fled the Corvidae. The garden was overgrown, choked with brambles and blanketed with a thick layer of snow. Beyond it, its jagged outlines softened by winter's touch, a pile of rubble that had once been a cottage lay still and silent.

'You OK?' Cay asked Jonathan.

He nodded, but deep down he wasn't so sure. It was

strange to be back finally. The cawing of a lone crow pulled him out of his pondering.

'Well then,' said Montgomery, leaving his gloves and goggles on the driver's seat. 'Where do we start?' He put his hands on his hips and grinned.

So much had changed over the course of the year. Before the attack of the Corvidae, the biggest problem Jonathan had had was how long he could put off stuffing his face with Easter eggs. Now he was trying to save the universe with the aid of a werewolf, a demon stuck in a cat's body and two relentlessly cheerful gargoyles. He returned Montgomery's grin.

'I remember Mum dragging me up an old coal chute round the back,' he said. 'Let's try that, see if there's enough room to get into the cellar.'

'Me first,' said Stubbs, forging ahead like a miniature snowplough.

They followed him to the rear of the house and sure enough there was the entrance to the coal chute, its wooden door hanging open. 'You gotta torch?' asked Stubbs. 'It's a bit dark down there.'

Jonathan nodded, and handed him a small penlight he'd stuffed in his pocket before leaving the vicarage. Stubbs popped it in his mouth and leaned into the ominous opening to the cellar.

'Ooh, it's a bit slip—'

He didn't get the chance to finish the sentence before he lost his grip on the rotten wood and disappeared headfirst down the chute. There was a grating sound followed by a crunch as he came to an abrupt stop somewhere below them.

'Stubbs? You all right?' Jonathan called out.

'Yep,' came a muffled reply. 'Watch that first step, it's a bit tricky.'

Bracing himself with his boots, Jonathan sat down and carefully slid after the gargoyle, closely followed by Cay, Elgar and Montgomery.

'Blimey,' said Elgar once they'd reached the bottom. 'Your dad did a number on this place, didn't he?'

Jonathan could only agree. The cellar was a mess of broken wood and masonry, but a way through had been cleared, probably when the Corvidae dug their way out and took Darriel with them. Retrieving the torch from Stubbs, he shone the light round the room. 'Right, let's have a look,' he said. 'Be careful, though, I don't know how stable this is. We don't want to get buried here if more stuff falls down.'

Clambering off the mound of cobwebbed coal, they followed Jonathan as he made his way deeper into the cellar.

'It's cold in here,' said Cay, rubbing her hands together.

'Yeah,' said Jonathan. 'Let's try to be quick. Have a look round; see if you can find anything interesting.'

They sifted through the debris, turning up random items of bric-a-brac, kitchen utensils, and the sodden remains of a sofa. Jonathan even found the crushed and mouse-nibbled husk of an Easter egg, still in its box. Just for a moment tears pricked the back of his eyes.

'What's this?' said Stubbs, clearing away rubble to reveal a box in the corner. Jonathan crouched on the floor next to the gargoyle. He saw that Stubbs had found an old trunk. It had been battered by falling bricks but hadn't been crushed. He lifted the lid to peer inside; it was full of baby clothes and toys, *his* baby clothes and toys.

'They kept them all,' he said.

'That's parents for you, Jonny,' said Elgar. 'Sentimental to a fault.'

'What's that?' said Cay, pointing to the inside of the lid where a pocket had been sewn into the lining.

Something had been tucked into the pocket and secured with a safety pin. Jonathan reached in and his fingers closed around an envelope. Carefully pulling it free, he turned it over and saw that a single word was written on it: *Jonathan*.

'Ooh, and indeed, err,' said Elgar. 'I wonder what's inside?'

With shaking fingers, Jonathan tore open the envelope to reveal a sheet of folded paper. He took it out and asked Cay to hold the torch while he read.

Dear Son

Part of me feels silly, writing this hoping that you will never have to read it, but of late I can't shake the feeling that the past is creeping up on us once again. We have moved so often and it has broken our hearts not to be able to tell you why. We will, though, when you're old enough to understand what is happening and where your true heritage comes from.

Regardless of anything else there is one thing I need to protect. It's a family heirloom of sorts. My father gave it to me and I wanted to give it to you. If you're reading this letter then the chances are that things didn't work out as I hoped, and so I've placed it here in the slim hope that if the worst happens you may find it and do what is necessary.

Your mother doesn't know about it, but it's for her own good and probably the good of everything, and I mean everything. Sorry to sound so cryptic, but I know you'll understand why in time. If there is one thing I hope you do, it's that you follow in my footsteps. You would be surprised what you can find if you just know where to look.

If this is the last time I get to write to you, then know that you are much loved and that you will never be alone.

Dad.

'Wow!' said Cay. 'That's really from Darriel, isn't it?'

Jonathan nodded. 'Yeah, it is.' His throat felt thick and he really had to fight the emotions that threatened to overwhelm him.

'What did he mean about a family heirloom?' asked Montgomery. 'Does he mean this book you've been hunting for? The one that Lucifer needs to fix everything?'

'I think he might,' said Jonathan. 'It's the only thing that makes sense.'

'Well, he could have been a little less mysterious,' said Elgar, 'or enclosed a map, and possibly a shovel.'

Jonathan smiled. 'He was clear enough for me,' he said. 'Dad could hardly explain what he was hiding and where he'd put it, could he? He didn't know if I'd ever see this letter or if someone else might find it. He told me what I need to know.'

'What did he say to you then?' asked Cay. 'Is it in code or something?'

'Sort of,' said Jonathan. 'He told me to follow in his footsteps and that's exactly what I'm going to do. Or rather, I already did.'

'Confused,' said Stubbs. 'Really, really confused.'

'I need to get over there,' said Jonathan, pointing to the wreckage of the cellar stairs. 'Give me a hand, will you?'

Keeping a wary eye on the bulging ceiling, they clambered over piles of fallen masonry, making sure they didn't dislodge any of the beams that stopped the rest of the cottage falling into the cellar. The stairs had been smashed to pieces, and large chunks of splintered wood covered what Jonathan was looking for. With the aid of the gargoyles he carefully moved the remains to one side.

Cay pointed the torch and gasped at what she saw. 'Not so cryptic when you know what to look for,' she said, patting Jonathan on the shoulder.

'No,' he said. On the floor in front of him was a patch of concrete, lighter in colour than the surrounding area. In the centre were two footprints, one much larger than the other. The larger footprint had the initial D underneath it, while the smaller had the initial J.

'Soon after we moved here a couple of years ago, Dad said he needed to fix a bit of the floor which was damaged by damp,' said Jonathan. 'While the cement was still wet he thought it'd be fun to leave our footprints there; so we did.'

'Ahh,' said Cay.

'And this helps us how?' asked Elgar.

'We look underneath it,' said Jonathan. 'I think Dad might have buried something here.' Manifesting his wings, Jonathan inserted the tips of the ribbons into the cement. Pulling as gently as he could, he felt it come away from the rest of the floor; miraculously the cast of the footprints remained intact. Placing it to one side, he looked into the hole he'd revealed. Nestled at the bottom was a square bundle, wrapped in thick plastic and sealed with tape.

'You've got to be kidding me,' said Elgar.

Jonathan lifted the bundle, and carefully tore away the wrapping to reveal what lay within. It was a large, leatherbound, hardback book secured with a brass lock. On the cover was a title embossed in gold lettering. It said *Kinder und Hausmarchen*, and at the bottom were the words *Jacob und Wilhelm Grimm*.

'It's just like you described it,' gasped Cay. 'I think it says *Children and Household Tales* in German.'

'How on earth do you know that?' said Elgar.

'Mr Peters has been teaching me,' said Cay. 'So, nyah!' She thumbed her nose at the cat.

Jonathan held the book in his hands, it was heavy and a shiver ran through him. 'There's something weird about it,' he said.

'Like what?' asked Elgar.

'I'm not sure,' said Jonathan. He touched the brass lock, fully expecting it not to budge, but it sprang open with a click.

'It's obviously meant for you,' said Stubbs. 'Open it then.'

With his heart in his mouth, Jonathan lifted the binding and looked inside; the type was in German with beautiful black and white illustrations.

'It's impressive all right,' said Cay. 'But it doesn't look like the book Lucifer needs.'

'No,' said Jonathan as he flicked through the pages. 'I don't get it. If this was so special why would Dad...' He stopped speaking and gasped as he realised what his father had been hiding. As he turned over page ninety-eight, the book of fairy tales finally gave up its secret. A recess had been cut out, and nestled within lay something that hummed with so much power it made the hairs stand up on the back of Jonathan's neck. No bigger than a notebook, two sheets of black glass lay flat together, and through them Jonathan could see the faint glow of a complex equation written in gold symbols.

'Is that what I think it is?' asked Cay.

Jonathan couldn't speak; he could feel the equation calling to him. It was as if it wanted to be read. He slammed the cover of Grimm's fairy tales shut, and sighed with relief as the urge to do the one thing Lucifer had told him explicitly *not* to do vanished.

'I think we can safely say that we've found *both* the books we're looking for,' he said, wiping sweat from his forehead.

'Well, this is brilliant!' said Montgomery. 'Let's get back home and show Sam. She'll be so happy. Mr Stubbs and I will go and get the car started.'

'I'll come with you,' said Cay. 'I can't feel my feet it's so cold.'

'I'll be along in a sec,' said Jonathan, staring at the book in his hands.

'Well, you were right after all,' said Elgar. 'Gabe would be proud.'

'So would Dad,' said Jonathan. 'It looks like Mum will get her Christmas present, too. I hope she doesn't mind that there's a big hole in the middle of it.'

'Nah, she'll be fine,' said Elgar. 'It should just be enough to stop her being permanently furious with us for joyriding.'

'Yeah,' said Jonathan, knowing he was going to get his ear bent regardless of the success of their search.

'Come on, sonny Jim,' said Elgar. 'Let's get going. With luck and a tailwind we might be back in time for lunch.'

Jonathan smiled at the cat. 'We've come a long way this year, haven't we, Elgar?'

'Yep,' said the cat. 'And hopefully there's a long way to go yet. Let's get this doohickey from the dawn of time back to someone who knows how to use it, shall we?'

Jonathan nodded, and getting to his feet he tucked the book under one arm and the cement cast under the other. 'Let's go, Cat,' he said, picking his way carefully across the cellar. They'd barely got halfway when they heard the sound of a car engine start, closely followed by a bang and a crunch.

'Oh, now what?' said Elgar. 'If they've pranged Mr Peters' car we're going to be in so much trouble.'

'Let's go and look,' said Jonathan, clambering awkwardly up the rickety coal chute and back into the snow. Arriving at the front of the cottage they saw what had caused the commotion; it did not make for pleasant viewing. Standing on the roof of the car was a tall, muscular demon dressed in strange patchwork armour. Cay was in front of him – restrained by his forearm – and with his free hand he held a wicked-looking knife to her throat. She was utterly terrified.

The gargoyles lay on the ground nearby, their hands and feet trussed with what looked like white rope. Behind them, was something that made Jonathan's blood run cold. It was a spider, and it was the size of a garden shed. It looked at him with eight black eyes, and clacked its fangs together while making an odd chittering noise.

'Finally,' said the demon. 'I'm Flay, and I was getting very bored waiting for you. I assume you've found the book of creation? That's a relief, my mistress *will* be pleased. Now, hand it over or I cut your friend's pretty little head off.'

Chapter 18

Arachnophobia

'Whoever you are, you don't want to do this,' said Jonathan. 'If you hurt my friends, you'll be sorry.'

'Don't threaten me, boy,' said Flay. 'Put the book down... NOW!'

Jonathan stared straight into the demon's eyes. There was no fear there, none at all, just controlled malice. Whoever he was this Flay was dangerous, and Jonathan knew that Cay's life hung in the balance. He felt a sharp stab on his shin, and looked down to see a spider scuttling away through the snow.

'It's mine,' said Elgar, chasing after it.

'Too slow,' said Flay, 'far too slow. I know what you're capable of so I thought I'd even the odds.'

'What have you...?' Jonathan gasped, and then the pain hit him; it was like acid poured into his veins.

'Try fighting me now,' said Flay. 'That venom is particularly unpleasant. It'll kill you unless you do something about it.'

Jonathan sank to his knees, his vision blurring as the poison rushed to his heart. Desperate to save Cay he focussed the power of his wings inward, struggling to remain conscious as he tried to heal himself.

'That was disappointingly easy,' said Flay, running the edge of his knife against Cay's cheek. 'I was hoping for more of a challenge, Jonathan, but I'm still going to add your skin to my collection.' He tipped his head back and laughed, then screamed as Cay sunk her teeth through his armour and into his arm. She'd changed into her wolf form, but at a speed Jonathan didn't think possible. One second she was there, the next Flay was holding an angry, red-furred werewolf. With a wrench of her head she tore free of his grip, her clothes falling shredded to the floor.

Flay snarled as the wound on his forearm gushed thick, black demon blood. 'You'll pay for that, little wolf!' he said, brandishing his knife.

Jonathan knew he had to act quickly. If he didn't, he'd be so busy fighting the poison that wracked his body he wouldn't be any use at all. Summoning his wings he flicked the ribbons towards the gargoyles, freeing them from the spider silk. As one they launched themselves upward, striking Flay as hard as they could. Knocked off balance, the demon lost his grip on the slippery roof of the car and tumbled backwards to land in the snow.

With extraordinary speed Flay leapt to his feet. Ducking

a blow from Stubbs, the demon slashed at Montgomery with his knife. Sparks flew, and the gargoyle screamed as the blade scored its way across his body. Jonathan couldn't believe it. The gargoyles weren't supposed to feel pain. What was that knife made of?

'Giant spider at nine o'clock,' shouted Elgar, and Jonathan turned to see it looming over him. He threw himself to one side, barely avoiding its fangs as they stabbed downward. Using what little energy he had left, Jonathan whipped his wings upward and sent the spider reeling across the garden. It skidded to a halt, dug its eight horribly hairy legs into the snow and launched itself at him once again.

Barely able to focus Jonathan struggled to his feet, the precious book and footprint cast under his arm. A red blur streaked in from his left and Cay leapt onto the spider's back, tearing at it with her jaws. It made a horrible whistling noise and rolled over, trying to crush her against the frozen ground. She leapt clear and put herself between the monster and Jonathan, teeth bared and a growl rumbling in her chest.

Giving Stubbs a kick that sent him reeling, Flay vaulted over the car and knocked Jonathan to the ground. The patch of cement spilled from his grasp and the demon glared at it with contempt. 'Humans,' he said, 'so pathetically sentimental. Let me show you what I think of your despicable race.' He raised his foot and grinned.

'No,' begged Jonathan. 'Please, don't.'

'Why?' said Flay. 'We're having so much fun.' Stamping down hard, he ground the precious memento of father and son beneath his heel.

Rage erupted inside Jonathan and he surged to his feet. 'You shouldn't have done that,' he said, heart hammering against his ribs. Fuelled by a terrible mix of pain and grief, he swung at Flay with his wing ribbons, wanting nothing more than to cut the demon in half.

It was only Flay's inhuman reflexes that saved him from instant death. Dodging the worst of the blow, the demon was lifted off his feet and slammed into the giant spider. In a tangle of limbs the two monsters crashed into the remains of the cottage, bringing what was left of the roof down on top of them.

'I think we should be off now,' said Elgar. 'This has all got a bit tense for my liking.'

Jonathan nodded. Clutching the book of fairy tales to his chest he staggered to the car and collapsed into the passenger seat. Elgar - bits of spider still clinging to his whiskers - jumped into the back.

'You OK, guys?' he asked the gargoyles as they assumed their driving positions.

'I've been better,' said Montgomery, starting the engine. 'Not a scratch in over a century and now I've got a damn great duelling scar across my chest.'

'Now you know how I feel when I get one of my ears knocked off,' said Stubbs from the footwell.

'Drive, please,' said Jonathan, groaning in agony as the spider venom burned its way through him.

'Consider it done,' said Montgomery. 'Floor it, Mr Stubbs.'

With a perfect handbrake turn, the Beetle swung out of the drive and shot off down the lane, slush arcing from its wheels.

'Where's Cay?' said Jonathan.

'She's coming!' said Elgar, lowering the rear window. Seconds later Cay exploded through the opening, turning the back seat into a tangle of red and black fur.

'Get us home, guys,' said Jonathan. 'Fast as you can.'

'Ha ha,' said Montgomery, slipping into full-on racing driver mode. 'I am gargoyle, hear me roar!'

'Roar away, Monty,' said Elgar, peering out of the back window. 'Uh oh, we've got incoming.'

Jonathan looked over his shoulder and saw a nightmare chasing them down the lane. It was the huge spider with Flay riding it like a jockey.

'Faster,' shouted Montgomery.

'The pedal is, as they say, to the metal,' replied Stubbs. 'Why couldn't Mr Peters have had an Aston Martin?'

'Junction coming up, hold on to something,' said Montgomery, wrenching the steering wheel to the left. Unable to grip the icy tarmac, the car slid across the junction and slammed into a hedge. The engine stalled and the gargoyle tried desperately to restart it. 'Come on, come on,' he muttered under his breath.

Jonathan watched in horror as the spider barrelled towards them. 'Now would be a good time, Monty,' he said.

'Got it!' said the gargoyle, as the engine mercifully burst into life.

'Huzzah!' came a shout from the footwell.

With smoke pouring from its tyres, the Beetle shot forward just in time to avoid being struck by two metric tons of outsized arachnid. Struggling to get its own grip on the road, the spider ploughed through the hedge and tumbled into the field beyond.

'Ha,' said Elgar from his perch on the rear shelf. 'Stitch that you eight-legged freak!'

'We're not home yet,' said Montgomery. 'Grab hold of something, everyone, this is gonna be bumpy. Full power, please, Mr Stubbs.'

'Okey dokey,' the gargoyle replied, working the pedals as fast as he could.

With his heart racing and sweat pouring down his face, Jonathan watched as Montgomery pushed the Beetle to its limits. Despite the snow and ice, the gargoyle handled the car like the racing driver he patently wanted to be.

'Our unpleasant new friends are back up and gaining!' said Elgar.

'Only another couple of miles and we'll be safe,' said Montgomery, the car bouncing from one verge to the other as the gargoyle struggled to keep control.

'We're not going to last another couple of miles,' said Elgar.

There was a thump on the roof, and Cay whined as Flay's blade punched through and began sawing.

'Oh great,' said Elgar. 'That knife of his doubles as a can-opener. Do something, Jonny!'

Jonathan took a deep breath and tried to concentrate. He was poisoned, hurtling along in a car being driven by gargoyles, and now a demon with a skinning fixation was trying to cut his way in. He tried to manifest his wings, but as soon as they flickered into life they vanished again. The pain was too great; he had no fight left.

'Almost there,' said Montgomery, just as Flay tore off the Beetle's roof.

With a sudden bang one of the front tyres exploded, sending the car into a spin.

'Brace for impact,' shrieked Montgomery, shutting his eyes.

Ploughing through snowdrifts, the Beetle came to an abrupt halt with its nose buried in a hawthorn hedge, right next to a red postbox. To add insult to injury the giant spider slammed into the rear of the car, ensuring there was no escape.

'Oh... dear,' said Elgar.

'We're almost home,' said Jonathan, opening the door and falling to the snow. Through watering eyes he saw Flay squatting in the middle of the road.

'So near and yet so far,' said the demon, scraping the tip of his knife across the icy surface. The noise made Jonathan's skin crawl. 'I'm going to take that book now,' he said, getting to his feet. 'But before I do, I'm going to carve out a piece of that wolf's hide to repair the damage she did to my armour. You can watch if you like, it'll be... educational.'

'I wouldn't be too sure of that,' said Montgomery.

'And what are you going to do about it?' asked Flay.

The gargoyle just grinned.

With an almighty roar, the familiar radiator grille of a classic Daimler hove into view and struck Flay head on. The demon flew over the roof and landed with a sickening crunch on the road behind, his body limp and still. The car skidded to a halt and two men climbed out.

'We leave you alone for a couple of days,' said Ignatius.

'And it all goes to hell in a handcart,' added Grimm. 'Is that a giant spider?'

'Yes,' said Elgar, hiding beneath Cay.

'I rather like spiders,' said Grimm, retrieving his favourite cricket bat from the Daimler's boot. 'Couldn't eat a whole one though, at least not in one sitting.'

Still clutching the book to his chest, Jonathan smiled in relief as Ignatius rushed over. 'Spider venom,' he said, pointing to his leg which was swollen and hot.

'Easy, lad,' said the vicar. 'Once you're inside the village you'll be fine. What's that you've got there? A book of fairy tales?'

Jonathan was about to explain what they'd found when he saw something terrible. Flay was no longer lying in the road, he was standing beside the Daimler with his knife at the ready.

'Well aren't you hard to kill,' said Grimm.

'Oh yes,' said Flay. 'I think you'll find that I'm more of a challenge than my useless Corvidae brethren. I see you're wearing one of their hats.' He pointed at Grimm's bowler. 'Mind if I take it?'

'You can try.'

'Oh, I shall,' said the demon.

'You can't fight us all, sonny Jim,' said Grimm. 'Not even with your pet over there. Admit it, you've lost.'

'Poor, deluded human,' spat Flay. 'You have no idea what you're up against.' He raised his head skyward and smiled. 'Welcome, Mistress,' he said. 'Welcome... Lilith.'

A figure dressed in crimson silk descended from the low cloud, riding the air on vast, bat-like wings. In her hands she gripped a spear that pulsed with virulent red energy.

'Give me the book,' she said, pointing at Jonathan.

He shook his head, barely able to think straight.

'Then you will all perish,' she said, 'and I'll take it from your cold, dead hands.' She raised the spear above her head, and Jonathan could feel the power building within it. The last Archdemon had come for them, and he couldn't even stand up.

Chapter 19

The Battle of Hobbes End: Part Three

A bolt of scarlet fire burst from the spear and shot toward Jonathan. He was in so much pain he didn't have the strength to be afraid. A starburst of molten evil exploded all around him, but there was no burning, no agony, and no death.

'You took your time,' said Ignatius.

Jonathan looked up to see Sammael hanging in the air, her gloss-black wing ribbons shrugging off the energy that would have incinerated them all.

'You dare attack my family!' she thundered.

'I was hoping you'd show up,' said Lilith, unfazed by Sammael's sudden appearance. 'I wanted you to witness the wonders I have wrought. Look closely, angel, do you see what I'm holding in my hands; do you recognise it?'

Sammael's eyes widened in horror. 'Gabriel and I forged that for Michael,' she gasped. 'What have you done, you monster?'

'I've made it... better,' said Lilith. 'It cuts so very, very well. It fought me for a long time, but I twisted its spirit until it had no choice but to serve me. Should I desire it, one cut from this blade and you will bleed and bleed until your veins run dry.'

Sammael recoiled from Lilith's words. 'I've called out to Lucifer,' she said. 'He's coming, and when he gets here we will destroy you for this outrage.'

'Oh, will you now,' said Lilith. 'You may be waiting some time, I'm afraid. Lucifer is currently... indisposed. In his absence, I'll use your brother's spear to reduce you to a smouldering corpse. Once that is done, I will take the book your great-nephew has gone to such lengths to find.'

Sammael glanced at Jonathan as he huddled on the ground with Ignatius. For the first time she saw what he had clutched in his hands.

'You will not,' she said, striking at Lilith with her wings. The Archdemon parried the blow with Michael's Spear, and Sammael screamed in agony as it severed one of her ribbons.

'Hurts, doesn't it?' said Lilith. 'You've no concept of how much power I've poured into this weapon; even your mighty wings are vulnerable to its blade. I've looked forward to this for such a long time, Sammael. Face your end at last!'

At a signal from Lilith the giant spider launched itself over the car while Flay dashed at Grimm. In seconds, battle raged.

'Get Jonathan and the book into Hobbes End!' shouted Sammael, desperately trying to avoid the spear's deadly blade. Ignatius slipped an arm under Jonathan's shoulders and lifted him to his feet, only to find his way blocked by venom-tipped fangs.

Cay leapt from the car and sank her teeth into one of the spider's legs. It swung her away, battering her against the side of the Beetle as she refused to let go.

'Take that,' said Stubbs, jumping onto the spider's head and punching it in the face as hard as he could. Montgomery followed Cay's example, grabbing hold of another leg and trying to pull it off. 'Get going!' he shouted at Ignatius. 'We'll deal with this.' The vicar nodded and, moving as fast as he could, he dragged Jonathan towards the forest entrance.

'Looks like it's just you and me,' said Flay, as he advanced on Grimm. 'Once you're dead I'll take a piece of *your* hide to add to my collection.'

'Isobel says no,' replied Grimm, taking a firm grip on his cricket bat.

'Does she now?' said Flay, and before Grimm could react the demon sprang at him with terrifying speed. Rook of the Corvidae had been fast, but Flay was another matter entirely. Grimm barely had time to parry the demon's knife before Flay was behind him and ready for another attack.

For the first time in his life Grimm knew fear. He'd been a doctor and a soldier and had faced enough enemies to know that Flay was death incarnate. Once again the demon rushed at him, and it was all Grimm could do to fend off blow after blow without leaving a mark of his own.

'You're quick for a human,' said Flay. 'But not quick enough. I'll try to make this as painful as possible for you.' His movements a blur, Flay ducked and cut a nasty gash across the big man's ribs. Grimm gasped in pain, swinging Isobel as hard as he could; he missed completely. This wasn't going to end well and Grimm knew it. He'd heard Sammael shout to Ignatius; all he could do was buy him enough time to get Jonathan inside the village boundary, even if it meant giving up his life to do it.

'Help me, Jonathan. Move your feet, lad,' begged Ignatius. The Hobbes End boundary was only twenty metres away, but it seemed so far.

Jonathan could hear Ignatius but his body felt like lead. The venom burned inside him and it took all his concentration to fight it. Clutching the heavy book to his chest he forced his feet to move and staggered onward, praying they would make it before someone got killed.

Bolting from his hiding place in the Beetle, Elgar raced up one of the spider's legs and pounced onto its hairy abdomen; tearing into it with his claws. It reared up underneath him, shaking Cay and Montgomery free and snapping at Stubbs with its fangs. Elgar howled and tried to hang on, but he lost his grip and slid off to land with a crunch in the snow. The spider stabbed down with one of its legs, and the cat barely managed to roll out of the way before it skewered him.

'Keep it busy!' shouted Stubbs, still doing his best to punch the monster in the head.

'I'm trying,' said Elgar. 'But I can't chew this one up and spit it out like the others. It's a bit big!'

Seeing Jonathan and Ignatius scrambling to safety, Lilith renewed her attacks on Sammael with a vengeance. Blood-red fire filled the air as bolt after bolt burst from the spear and arced towards the angel. Weakened by her injuries, it was all Sammael could do to fend them off with her wings. She could feel the malice the Archdemon had poured into the weapon. One cut from that awful blade meant a slow and painful death.

'Hurry!' she screamed at Ignatius.

Lilith chose her moment and flew past the angel, diving at full speed towards Jonathan. In desperation, Sammael wrapped the Archdemon in her wing ribbons, pinning her arms to her sides and pulling her from the sky. As they plummeted down, Sammael reached out and grabbed her brother's spear in both hands, trying to wrench it from Lilith's grasp. The second she touched it she was filled with a pain that not only burned her hands but tore into her soul. She and Gabriel had laboured over this weapon for days, creating something that Michael could use in the defence of Heaven. In her brother's hands it had been extraordinary, but now it was filled with rage, corrupted by whatever poison Lilith had crammed into it. She could feel no trace of Michael, just a seething mass of hate and a desire to cut and cut deep.

Sammael's hands smoked but she refused to let go, and in a flailing tangle of wings and limbs they slammed onto the roof of the Daimler, crushing the car like a giant hammer.

'Oh, come on!' said Grimm, shielding his eyes from flying glass.

'Now you know how I feel every time I lose an ear,' said Stubbs, still battering away at the spider's head.

Flay came at Grimm once more, and yet again the demon dodged the crushing edge of Isobel to score a thin red line across Grimm's body. 'Death of a thousand cuts, old man,' said Flay, readying himself for another charge. 'I'll teach you to run me over with your car.'

'You're a tough one, I'll give you that,' panted Grimm. His face didn't show it but he knew this fight wasn't going to last much longer. Flay was toying with him and there was only so much damage he could take. From the corner of his eye Grimm could see Jonathan and Ignatius were almost at the entrance to Hobbes End. Taking a deep breath he raised Isobel once more and beckoned to the demon. If he was going down, then he would go down knowing his friends had reached safety.

Cay growled and snapped at the spider, dodging the deadly fangs and trying to avoid being struck by one of its legs.

'Running on fumes here,' said Montgomery, his grip on the spider failing.

'I hear ya,' said Stubbs, his punches slowing with every blow.

It wasn't tiring, but *they* were. The cold was sapping their strength, and Lilith's demonic will drove her minion to attack with relentless fervour. Cay knew that so much activity was draining the gargoyles. They'd fought the Corvidae and then Baal during the spring and summer when the sun shone bright, but this was midwinter, and Gabriel hadn't designed Montgomery and Stubbs for sustained exertion. Without sufficient sunlight to recharge them they were going to fall asleep, and there was nothing anyone could do about it.

Sensing weakness, the spider shook itself free of the gargoyles. With sweeping blows from its legs, it smashed

Montgomery and Stubbs through the hedge and into the forest that surrounded Hobbes End. Without the energy to fly, the gargoyles ploughed into the trees with despairing wails.

'Cay, we need to–' Elgar was thrown into the air as the spider bucked beneath him like a rodeo bull. Cay tried to attack but was knocked aside with a blow that left her head ringing.

'Almost there, Jonathan,' gasped Ignatius. 'Just a few more steps and we'll be safe.' Lilith gave a furious shriek as she saw her prey escaping, and Jonathan turned his head towards her. With a vicious heave, Lilith wrenched the spear from Sammael's grip and swung it upward, cutting through another of the Archangel's wing ribbons. Sammael screamed in pain, tumbling from the roof of the car as her grip on Lilith failed. Free at last, the Archdemon drew back the spear and launched a huge bolt of fire directly at Jonathan and Ignatius.

With the last of his strength Jonathan threw himself forwards, pulling the vicar down with him. His vision filled with scarlet as a wall of fire exploded just centimetres from his feet. Demonic energy crackled and hissed, scorching the air, but none of it reached him; with that last step he'd crossed the border of Hobbes End and found sanctuary.

Lilith howled in fury, hammering at the invisible shield

that protected the village, but it was in vain. Gabriel's defences held. Nothing evil could enter Hobbes End, and the power that flowed from the spear was as evil as anything Jonathan had ever felt.

'Ha, made it!' shouted Ignatius, grabbing hold of Jonathan's jacket and dragging him further into the forest.

Flay turned to look at his mistress, so Grimm took advantage of the momentary distraction and ran. Rather than face the volcanic fire of Lilith's wrath, he dived at the hawthorn hedge and ploughed straight through it. It tore at his skin, but compared to the injuries inflicted by Flay the pain was nothing.

Seeing that Jonathan and the book were safe, Elgar jumped onto Cay's back. 'Hi ho, Silver,' he shouted as they shot after Grimm, making good use of the hole he'd made in the hedge.

With the skin on her hands still burning, Sammael launched herself into the air and fled, too. Summoning one last bolt of utter hatred from the spear, Lilith sent it screaming towards the angel. Just before Sammael reached safety, red fire blasted her from the sky. Jonathan could only watch in horror as his great-aunt's body fell somewhere amongst the trees.

Jonathan looked at Lilith as she stood on the remains of the Daimler, pointing at him with the spear. For a moment he didn't understand what she was doing, but then the entrance to the forest road was filled with the awful sight of the giant spider as it rushed towards him, straight through the village's defences.

'How?' Jonathan gasped.

'It's not evil,' said Ignatius. 'It's just some mindless creature doing the bidding of its mistress. The village doesn't see it as a threat!' The vicar redoubled his efforts but his feet slipped in the snow and he fell heavily.

The spider reared up, ready to tear them apart with its fangs when it suddenly froze. A deep, bass rumble started, and a dark shape spread above Jonathan and Ignatius as they lay sprawled on the frozen ground. Through unfocussed eyes Jonathan could see the weak sunlight reflecting on metal scales, and there, right over his face, was a plaque engraved with the letter 'G'. It was Brass.

'Say hello to my little friend,' said Elgar, running over with Cay at his side.

With her foreclaws placed protectively either side of Jonathan and Ignatius, the dragon inhaled. Thrusting her head forward, she opened her jaws to spew forth a torrent of flame with the force of a jet engine. It hit the spider full in the face, tearing through its bulbous body and reducing it to ash in the blink of an eye. But the dragon didn't stop there. Brass' fury surged onward, hitting the ruined Daimler where Lilith still stood and igniting the petrol tank. The car exploded, and Brass threw up her wings for cover as bits of smoking metal rained down around them.

Silence descended, and folding her wings against her body Brass settled back on her haunches, a pleased look on her face. In front of her, eight thoroughly-crisped giant spider legs stood upright with nothing to support them. One by one they tottered and fell, hitting the snow with a sizzle.

'And that, children,' said Elgar happily, 'is why we don't play with matches.'

'Lilith?' said Jonathan.

'She's escaped,' said Ignatius. 'Along with that demon that was tearing strips off Grimm.'

'I heard that,' said Grimm, tottering out of the forest with an unconscious Sammael cradled in his arms. 'I was just lulling him into a false sense of security.'

'That would explain why you look as though you've been put through a blender,' said Ignatius. 'We're going to have to go and buy more bandages.'

There was a snapping of twigs, and the gargoyles crawled out of the forest on their hands and knees.

'I'm all hurty,' groaned Montgomery.

'Me too,' said Stubbs. 'At least none of my ears got knocked off this time, which is a bonus.'

'Well, Jonathan,' said Ignatius, 'once you're patched up I think you need explain why you were out joyriding with the gargoyles, and why you have a German copy of Grimm's fairy tales clutched to your chest.'

'Not much of a happy-ever-after, is it?' said Grimm, staring at the remains of his Daimler. 'You realise that the Christmas presents from the boot are now spread in smoking bits over a wide area.'

'Don't tell Mum,' said Ignatius. 'She spent ages knitting us scarves and jumpers.'

'I've missed you guys,' said Elgar. 'We do have one problem, though.'

'Such as,' said Jonathan.

'How do we tell Mr Peters his car is now a convertible?'

Chapter 20

Aftermath

Jonathan opened his eyes and groaned. There wasn't an inch of him that didn't hurt in some way. He was in his room at the vicarage, although he couldn't remember how he'd got there. He sensed that the spider venom was finally gone from his body, but it had come close to killing him; only the power contained within his incredible wings had saved his life.

'Ah, he awakes,' said Elgar from the windowsill. 'Back in the land of the living after a day's sleep. You're looking less rubbish than you did.'

'Thanks,' said Jonathan, propping himself on his elbows. 'I think I must have passed out after Brass saved us. Who put me to bed?'

'Your mum did,' said the cat. 'She threw a right wobbly when Ignatius dragged you in. There was much wailing and gnashing of teeth until Grimm calmed her down with a cup of Earl Grey.'

'Oh no,' said Jonathan. 'I'm in so much trouble, aren't I?'

'Well, yes,' said Elgar. 'At least you didn't come back empty-handed, that might save you from being grounded for the rest of your life.'

Jonathan sighed and slumped back on his pillows. 'Is Sam OK? I couldn't tell with her being carried by Grimm and everything.'

Elgar paused and Jonathan's heart sank.

'She'll live,' said Elgar, 'but she took one hell of a battering. That spear Lilith was using belonged to Michael.'

'Yeah,' said Jonathan. 'I heard what Sam said when she was fighting.'

'Whatever Lilith has done to it is really bad news,' said Elgar. 'It's like she's stuffed it full of concentrated evil. That final blast did Sammael a lot of damage. She didn't see it coming and couldn't get her wings up in time to protect herself.'

'Will she be all right?'

'Michael seems to think so, but it'll take time. She's resting over at the windmill.'

Jonathan shook his head. 'At least we managed to save the book of creation. I dread to think what Lilith would have done if she'd got her hands on it. How did she know we were looking for it anyway?'

'No idea,' said Elgar. 'Oh, by the way, his royal Luciferness is over at the windmill too. He has custody of said book and wants to talk to you urgently.'

'Oh great,' said Jonathan. 'What about everyone else?'

'Well, Brass is back snoozing in the pond after her foray into giant arachnid incineration.'

'I missed seeing that when the first squid monster attacked,' said Jonathan. 'Cay was right, it was very impressive.'

'Brass is certainly full of surprises,' said Elgar. 'Another reason to keep on her good side. As for Miss Forrester, she's a bit bruised but otherwise she's fine, tough little lupine that she is. She's currently under house arrest; you know what her parents are like.'

'Oops,' said Jonathan, covering his face with his hands. 'I'm going to have to go over and apologise, aren't I?'

'Probably, although you may want to wait until her mum's calmed down a bit. She is not best pleased. And Mr Peters wants a word about his roofless car. I don't think he's angry but he'd rather nobody know that he just let you take it.'

'Anything else I need to sort out?' said Jonathan.

'You need to chat with your mum, Ignatius and Grimm. They're all waiting in the kitchen with serious looks on their faces.'

'Do you actually have any good news?'

'This may cheer you up,' said Elgar. 'Have a look out of the window.'

Jonathan swung his legs out of bed and joined the cat.

'After all their exertions, Monty and Stubbs are gonna be asleep for days,' said Elgar, 'so I took the liberty of adding some festive decorations while they couldn't do anything about it.'

Peering through the frosty glass, Jonathan saw that Elgar had placed a green and red elf-hat on each of the gargoyles' heads.

'What do you think?'

Jonathan couldn't help but laugh. 'I think they'll be furious.'

The bedroom door banged open and a patently livid Savantha strode in. 'So you're up?' she said snippily.

'Um, hi, Mum,' said Jonathan. 'I can explain.'

'I have no idea how you convinced Mr Peters to let you take his car,' said Savantha as she led Jonathan into the kitchen. 'Have you any idea how stupid that was? You could all have been killed!'

'Well, I didn't know for sure whether the book of creation was in our old cottage,' protested Jonathan. 'And I had no idea that Lilith was after it either.'

'That's not the point!' shouted Savantha.

'And I wanted to get you a Christmas present. You said you gave that book of Grimm's fairy tales to Dad. I wanted to find it and give it back to you. You'd never have let me go if I'd asked, would you?'

Savantha went quiet and wrapped her arms around her son. 'You... are... infuriating,' she said. 'But I love you.'

'My car got blown up,' said Grimm. 'I know it's not your fault, but I'm going to moan about it anyway.'

'We'll get you a new one,' said Ignatius, looking up from the morning paper. 'You know Monty has always wanted to drive an Aston Martin.'

'Ooh!' said Grimm. 'Can we? An old DB5 like James Bond used to drive?'

'We'll see,' said Ignatius. 'You'd better get over to the windmill, Jonathan. Lucifer's pacing a groove in the floor waiting for you. Have you recovered from that spider bite?'

'I think so,' he said. 'I feel rubbish but hopefully it's out of my system. If I ever get my hands on Lilith there'll be trouble.'

'You'll stay right here inside Hobbes End until Lucifer says it's safe to leave,' ordered Savantha. 'We have no idea what she's up to and, until we do, nobody goes anywhere. Is... that... clear?'

'And a merry Christmas to us all,' said Elgar. 'That reminds me, I still haven't written out my present list. I'd quite like a smartphone but texting is a tad tricky without...'

'Yeah, yeah, everything's so difficult without opposable thumbs,' said Jonathan, rolling his eyes. 'Come on, let's get over to the windmill and see what Lucifer wants.'

Crossing the green, they could see Mr Peters throwing a tarpaulin over his decapitated Beetle. Jonathan decided he had to go and apologise.

'I'm so sorry, Mr Peters,' he said. 'I wasn't expecting us to be attacked by an Archdemon, her personal assassin and a giant spider.'

'Hmm,' said Mr Peters. 'You do have a point. Still, the important thing is that you are all safe, yes?'

Jonathan nodded, happy the old man was taking it so well.

'And please call me Vladimir. Mr Peters sounds too formal, don't you think? As for the car, I was thinking of trading it in for something sportier anyway.'

'You should go and speak to Grimm,' said Elgar. 'He's pondering the very same thing.'

'I may just do that,' said Mr Peters. 'Oh, and I take it everyone still thinks you fibbed your way into borrowing my car?'

'Yeah,' said Jonathan.

'Best we keep it that way, eh?' His dark eyes twinkled beneath the brim of his hat.

'Done, Vladimir,' said Jonathan, shaking Mr Peters' hand.

The old man smiled. 'You should go and see Cay later. Her parents seem rather displeased that she has once again been magnificent and stupid.'

'I'm so doomed,' said Jonathan.

'Ah, it'll be fine. Worse things happen at sea and all that.'

'I doubt it,' said Elgar. 'Best we get going. Lucifer's waiting.'

Saying goodbye to Mr Peters, they continued on their way.

'We did recover the big bang book,' said Elgar. 'That's got to count for something, hasn't it? Imagine how angry his nibs would be if Lilith had got her mitts on it?'

'Yep,' said Jonathan. 'I still can't figure out how she knew we'd be there. Maybe Lucifer will know?'

'One can but hope,' said Elgar. 'Come on; let's hear what he has to say.'

They entered the windmill to find Michael and Lucifer sitting by the fire. Between them, on the table, lay the rather battered copy of Grimm's fairy tales, and next to it, resting on a bed of silk cloth, lay the book of creation.

'Well,' said the fallen angel. 'Haven't you been busy?'

'We got you your book back, what more do you want?' said Elgar. 'How about a little appreciation?'

'Make no mistake, I *am* very appreciative,' said Lucifer. 'Once again, Jonathan, you impress me with your ability to get things done. Now we have the book, I may be able to stop these rips appearing. Hopefully we can then look forward to a time where we don't get invaded by any more... how did you put it, Elgar? Tentacle boys?'

'I'm all for that,' said the cat. 'Do you think you can use *the book* without wrecking creation then?'

'We shall see,' said Lucifer. 'However, we appear to have a new problem.'

'Lilith,' said Jonathan, slumping into an armchair. 'How did she know what I was doing? What does she want with the book?'

'More importantly, what the hell has she done to my spear?' said Michael, his face thunderous. 'How dare she! When I'm back to full strength I'm going to cut her into little chunks, just see if I don't.' The wooden arms of Michael's chair splintered under the pressure of his hands.

'Steady on,' said Elgar.

'I will not,' shouted Michael. 'Sam is upstairs and barely alive, all because that miserable Archdemon stole my weapon and corrupted it. Apparently a single cut from its blade will now be fatal to anyone, including all of us. It wasn't designed to do such an appalling thing. It's vile!'

'Yes, Michael,' said Lucifer. 'It is. I assume she found it after your near-death experience and worked her evil into it for centuries. My question is, why?'

Michael sat fuming, but Jonathan could understand his anger.

'The spear is like me,' he said. 'It's now got angel and demon inside it, but Lilith forced it to serve her, just like Belial tried to force me to serve him, become a weapon he could use.'

'I know,' said Michael. 'You had free will and you chose well, but for all its power my spear is just an object; it couldn't resist Lilith forever. Not only is it lost to me, but it's now in the hands of the one being I would rather it wasn't.'

'We've bumped off two Archdemons so far,' said Elgar. 'One more shouldn't be a problem, should it?'

'I don't know,' said Lucifer. 'I need to figure out what she's up to before I decide whether to move against her. I don't want to start a war right at this minute. Healing creation comes first.'

'Why didn't you come to help us when Lilith attacked?' asked Jonathan. 'Sam said she'd called for you.'

'She did,' replied Lucifer. 'I was just about to leave my castle when something bit me on the leg. I spent the next few hours writhing in agony, much to the alarm of poor Delius. Hence my absence at a fight that had I attended, would likely have resulted in Lilith being handed her entrails on a plate. I gather you had a similar experience, Jonathan?'

'Yeah,' he said. 'She obviously wanted me out of the way to make it easier to grab the book.'

'Gotcha!' said Elgar, pouncing on something that scuttled across the floor.

'Bring me that!' ordered Lucifer.

The cat dutifully hopped onto his lap and dropped something into his outstretched hand. Jonathan saw it was a small spider; well, small compared to the one that had chased them along the B1149 north of Norwich.

'Stay,' said Lucifer, pointing a finger at the quivering arachnid that crouched in his palm. 'So that's what she's been up to. You can see and hear me, can't you, Lilith? You've had your little minions creeping about, spying on us, haven't you?'

The spider tried to run, but Lucifer's will held it frozen.

'Well, Lilith, queen of the silk garden. I see *you* now!'

Lucifer made a fist and squeezed, reducing the spider to a pulp which oozed between his fingers.

Sitting by the scrying pool, Flay watched in horror as his mistress clapped her hands to her face and screamed in pain. 'I can't see,' she cried. 'I'm blind!'

Flay put his hand to her shoulder to steady her but she slapped it away. 'Don't touch me,' she hissed, fumbling for the haft of Michael's Spear. It pulsed under her touch, and her breathing steadied.

'Oh, you will pay for that, Lucifer,' she snarled. 'You will pay so very dearly!'

'What did you just do?' asked Jonathan.

'I gave her a slap across the face,' said Lucifer. 'If she thinks she can have her filthy little arachnids scampering about, spying for her and biting us she's sadly mistaken. She won't be able to use any more of her minions here for a while.'

'That would explain why there's been so many of the little critters about the place,' said Elgar.

There was a gentle pattering sound as hundreds of dead spiders fell from the rafters to land on the tiled floor.

'Jackpot!' said Elgar, scooping them into his mouth and giving them all a good chew before spitting them out.

'That is quite disgusting,' said Jonathan.

'I still don't get why Lilith was after that book,' said Michael, pointing at the table. 'Did she want to stop us fixing creation or something?'

'It doesn't make any sense,' said Lucifer, rubbing his face. 'That venom has got my mind all fuzzy; I can't think straight.'

'When will you use the book?' asked Jonathan.

'As soon as possible,' he replied. 'I'm not letting it out of my sight. I'll stay here with Sam and Michael. Hobbes End is as safe a place as any despite the flaws in its defences. I don't think Gabriel expected to be dealing with a spider invasion.'

'What if Lilith has constructs of her own?' asked Jonathan, remembering the awful attack by Baal and the Cherubim. The Archdemon had corrupted Gabriel's hollow angels, three perfect killing machines; they'd almost destroyed the village. 'You know Hobbes End doesn't see something as a threat unless it's actually evil.'

'It's a valid concern,' said Lucifer. 'But unless Lilith does something immediately she'll be too late. I doubt she wants to confront both of us at the same time. Once I've patched up creation, that book is going straight back to Uriel's tomb where it can rest for all eternity.'

Jonathan nodded, hoping Lucifer was right.

'And once the book's safe we can go and get my spear back,' said Michael. 'I'm not having Lilith use it to cut anyone, especially if it means they'll bleed to death.'

Jonathan gasped. Michael was right, if Lilith used that spear to cut anyone, or *anything*, the wound would be fatal if she chose it.

'Oh my God,' he said, as the puzzle pieces fell into place. 'I think I know what Lilith wants to do!'

Chapter 21

Heartbreaker

'We've been conned,' said Jonathan. 'We've done what she wanted all along. I knew there was something wrong about those rips. I knew it! They're not random. They're not caused by the damage Sammael did when she destroyed Baal.'

'What?' said Lucifer, his face grave.

'It's all adding up,' said Jonathan. 'You said you didn't think Michael calling out to us just after that first rip appeared was coincidence.'

'Yes.'

'You were right, it wasn't. Michael, you don't remember the nightmare you had that first night after we found you, but I do. You were shouting about things coming apart, threads being cut, something that was very, very sharp.'

Michael's eyes went wide and his mouth fell open. 'It's her, isn't it? She's using my spear to cut holes in the weave of creation, let those monsters in from outside. I was hovering between life and death in Raphael's tower, but I could still feel something terrible was happening, something connected to me. That's why I called out to you. I wanted to help.'

'Exactly,' said Jonathan.

'I really am getting old,' said Lucifer. 'I was so sure the rips were caused by Sammael.'

'Which is what Lilith wanted us to think,' said Jonathan. 'When I helped Sam to close that rip in the forest there was something about it that didn't feel right. I'd forgotten about it until now. It was the way the threads of reality looked. They hadn't just frayed and come apart; they'd been cut, severed cleanly. I had the same feeling about the rip outside Lucifer's castle. It was Lilith, I know it.'

'But why would she do that?' asked Michael. 'Why would she start cutting holes in reality and letting monsters in?'

Lucifer clapped his hand to his forehead. 'I'm so stupid!' he growled. 'Jonathan's completely right. Lilith played us like a violin. She knew what I would do if I thought creation was at risk, she knew I'd want to save it and that the only way of doing so would be to find that book! *That* was what she wanted all along, for us to fetch it so she could take it from us.'

'Why does she want it so badly?' asked Michael, scratching his head. 'She can't use it without destroying creation and herself along with it.'

'Not unless she's already cut reality to pieces,' said

Jonathan. 'Not unless she opens up a rip that we can't repair, and stands by and watches as everything and everyone dies. Once those things from outside have torn it all apart, she'd have the means to restart creation. No more Heaven, no more Hell, no more Earth, just a brand new universe with her in charge.'

Lucifer looked as though he was going to explode. His entire body shook with rage. 'She... wouldn't... dare!'

'I think she would,' said Jonathan. 'She saw what happened to Belial and Baal. She's not going to bother with some war she can't win. She wants to undo everything and start again.'

'Well, it's a good job we stopped her getting her hands on the book,' said Michael.

Lucifer nodded, breathing deeply as he tried to regain his composure. 'You really are a chip off the old block, Jonathan. Gabriel would have known what was happening from day one. He knew how dangerous the book would be in the wrong hands and he hid it so well. Now we've gone and dug it up and put everything, and I mean *everything*, at risk.'

'So what do we do?' asked Jonathan.

'Two things,' said Lucifer. 'First, we put the book back inside Uriel's tomb, and then we go after Lilith with a vengeance. I'm not leaving her to run around causing havoc with that spear. Sooner or later she might decide to destroy creation out of sheer spite.'

'I agree,' said Michael.

'Me too,' said Jonathan. All was quiet for a moment and then a faint cry made him jump. 'It's Sam,' he said, running for the stairs. He shot up them two at a time and burst into her bedroom. His great-aunt was lying on her side, her torso wrapped in bandages and her white hair flowing over the pillows like a waterfall. Her face was lined with pain, and beads of sweat trickled from her forehead and on to the sheets.

Jonathan knelt by the bed, taking her hand as she held it out to him. 'I... heard... you... talking,' she said, her voice tight and hoarse.

'Would you like some water?' Jonathan asked.

The angel nodded. Picking up a glass from the bedside table, Jonathan held it to her lips, tipping it gently so she didn't choke.

'We know what Lilith's up to,' he said. 'We've stopped her.'

Sammael shook her head. 'It won't be over until she's dead. It never is. If she can contemplate destroying everything, all those billions and billions of lives just so she can play god, then she is truly mad. She will never stop, Jonathan. She will never stop trying until either she, or all of us, have stopped breathing.'

In his heart Jonathan knew that Sammael was right; Lilith had shown her true colours. She had the spear and could tear a wound in creation that would devour all light and life. But *they* had the book of creation. It was stalemate. For now.

'We're going to put the book back in Uriel's tomb,' said Jonathan. 'Only you, me or Michael can open it. That should keep it safe, even if Lilith could get inside Heaven.'

Sammael gave him a weak smile and touched his face. 'So much for finally having a quiet life, eh?'

They heard muffled voices from downstairs. 'I wonder who that is?' said Jonathan. Footsteps approached and two figures appeared at the bedroom door. One was Ignatius. He had an exasperated look on his face but he was smiling. At his side stood a small, slim woman in her eighties, wrapped in a winter coat. Her grey hair was tied in a bun and her green eyes twinkled with life. She looked at Sammael with an expression of total and unconditional love.

'Mama,' the old woman said, kneeling by Sammael and laying her head gently on the angel's chest. Sammael wrapped her arms round the woman and hugged her, tears pouring down her face.

'Constance,' she whispered. 'My daughter, you're home.'

'I heard you'd been hurt so I came,' said Constance, the faint trace of an eastern European accent still audible in her voice. 'I got a taxi.'

'From Devon?' said Sammael.

'Ignatius kindly paid the driver.'

Jonathan glanced at the vicar and understood the look on his face. That must have been some taxi fare.

'I'll leave you two alone,' he said.

Constance smiled at him, and for a second he saw her through Gabriel's eyes, a shy little girl in a pretty dress. 'We'll talk,' she said. 'I want to hear your story.'

'I'd like that,' said Jonathan.

'Come on, lad,' said the vicar. 'I need some tea.'

They walked downstairs leaving Constance and Sammael to share some private time.

'If there's one thing you need to learn about my mother,' said Ignatius, 'it's that she does what she wants. When I told her what had happened there was no stopping her from coming up. I thought it was too risky under the circumstances, but there you go.'

'It'll be nice having her here for Christmas, won't it?' asked Jonathan.

'Yes,' said Ignatius. 'It will. I just need to find the right moment to tell her that the presents she made for Grimm and me got blown up.'

They joined Lucifer, Michael and Elgar by the fire. In his hands, Lucifer held the book that had been the source of so much trouble. Jonathan could sense the vast power radiating from it, like an unborn star trapped within the glass pages.

'I'd forgotten what this felt like,' said Lucifer, gently

stroking it with his fingers. 'Perhaps we should keep it to hand in case Lilith does something really stupid? I could use it to heal the damage she does.'

Jonathan met the fallen angel's eyes. 'Don't,' he said. 'It's too dangerous. What if you started using it and found you couldn't stop? What if you ended up reading the whole equation? You know what would happen.'

Lucifer sighed and smiled at him. 'I must be getting soft,' he said. 'Take it back to Uriel's tomb. Lock it away where it'll be safe from Lilith and other... temptations.'

'I will,' said Jonathan. 'Once I've seen Cay. I won't be long. I just want to make sure she's all right.'

'I'll come with you,' said Elgar. 'I want to see her too.'

'Actually, Cat, do you mind staying behind for a moment?' asked Lucifer. 'I want to have a word?'

'Um, OK,' said Elgar. 'I'll see you over at Cay's, Jonny.'

Jonathan nodded, wondering what Lucifer was going to say.

'I've got something for you, Elgar,' said Lucifer once Jonathan had left.

'It's not a flea collar, is it?'

'No,' said Lucifer, 'just this.' He handed Elgar a slim package bound in festive wrapping paper.

'Ooh! A crimbo present. Will it be what I've always wanted? I haven't got you anything, no offence.'

'None taken,' said Lucifer. 'And as for it being what you've always wanted, well, you'll see on Christmas day, won't you? No peeking.'

'Now would I?' said Elgar.

'Yes, you would,' said Ignatius. 'I'll take it back to the vicarage and keep it under armed guard.'

'Spoilsport,' grumped Elgar.

Jonathan trudged across the green. His body still ached but he could feel his strength returning. He didn't feel particularly festive, especially after what Sammael had just said. Lilith was the biggest threat they'd ever faced and they'd only just realised it. Once he'd replaced the book in Uriel's tomb, he would try and figure out how to deal with the Archdemon. He knew deep down that a confrontation was inevitable, but he still wished there was an alternative.

'You look better,' said Cay.

Jonathan snapped out of his brooding to see her leaving the village shop.

'I'm on parole,' she said, running over. 'I was being very grumpy and annoying, so Mum let me out of the house as long as I promised not to do anything daft.'

'I really should apologise to her,' said Jonathan. 'It was my idea to go joyriding.'

'Ah, she knows what I'm like,' said Cay. 'You hardly twisted my arm, did you?'

'There is that,' said Jonathan, smiling at her.

'That was a fight and a half, wasn't it?' said Cay. 'It was all touch and go for a bit.'

'I wish I could have joined in,' said Jonathan. 'I might have stopped Sam getting so badly hurt.'

'How is she?'

'She'll recover,' said Jonathan. 'But it'll take a while. The evil Lilith poured into Michael's Spear did a lot of damage. Constance is with her though.'

'Constance is here?' said Cay. 'Oh, that's lovely. I haven't seen her in ages. Is she staying for Christmas?'

'I think so,' said Jonathan. 'I'm looking forward to getting to know her.'

'She's sweet,' said Cay. 'You'll like her. Look, I'm gonna go and ask if Vladimir will take me to see the cubs again. Want to come along?'

'I'd love to,' said Jonathan, 'but I've got an errand to run. I'm taking the book back to Heaven, to get it tucked away safe and sound. I just need to grab some lunch first. I haven't eaten anything in ages.'

'Fair enough,' said Cay. 'See you later, yeah?'

Jonathan nodded and watched his friend run off. He stood still for a moment, looking at the village sitting happily under its blanket of snow. Monty and Stubbs slept on their gateposts, Brass was curled up at the bottom of the pond, and beneath it all he could hear the song of his grandfather's wings, etched into the earth under his feet. It was comforting. This had been a year of struggle, loss and triumph. The price had been high, but he finally had a home, and more family around him than he could ever have imagined. Lilith was still out there, but for now he wanted to have a normal Christmas: presents, carols, snowball fights and far too much chocolate. That wasn't too much to ask was it?

Lilith knelt by her scrying pool, her hands clasped to her face as she rocked slowly to and fro. Flay stood to one side, knowing that to disturb his mistress might result in his incineration. After what seemed like an age, Lilith stood up and took Michael's Spear from its onyx cradle.

'So be it,' she said. 'The end begins now.' Holding the spear at arm's length, she chanted in a language that Flay didn't understand. The spear pulsed with bloody crimson light, and black smoke rose from Lilith's hands as she poured so much malice into the weapon it even burned her. The runes etched into the spear's haft flared into brilliance and Flay took an involuntary step back.

Lilith's chanting reached fever pitch and she raised the spear above her head, blade uppermost; the tip so bright that Flay had to shield his eyes.

'I will show you what suffering means,' she howled. 'I will show you all!' And with nothing but hate in her heart she began to cut.

Sitting at the kitchen table with Savantha, Jonathan munched happily on a toasted sandwich.

'I'm very proud of you, you know,' she said.

'Thanks, Mum,' he said, smiling at her.

'Your father and your grandfather would say the same if they were here.'

'They are here,' said Jonathan, 'always.'

Savantha nodded. 'I miss Darriel,' she said. 'And you go and do something so stupid and so sweet as to find me that copy of Grimm's fairy tales for a Christmas present. You have no idea how much that means to me, my lovely boy.'

'I think I do,' said Jonathan, giving her a hug.

'We are finally home, my son. We are all together and it'll soon be Christmas Eve. I'm quite looking forward to the carol service in the church. Grimm has been busy decorating it with holly and mistletoe; it looks quite beautiful.'

'I'll go and see when I get back from Heaven,' he said.

'That sounds such a strange thing for my son to be saying,' said Savantha. '*When I get back from Heaven*. I wonder where life will take us now, Jonathan?'

'Who knows,' he said. 'Hopefully there won't be any more chaos. I've had enough of that to last me a lifetime.'

'Me too,' said Savantha. 'Me too.'

Stuffing the last of his lunch into his mouth, Jonathan got up and kissed his mother on the cheek. 'Right, better go and put the book back where it belongs,' he said. 'No need to worry about me, nothing's going to happen.'

Savantha smiled at him. 'I'll have the kettle on,' she said.

Jonathan couldn't help but chuckle at the gargoyles adorned with their elf-hats as he walked down the drive. Elgar might have had his faults, but lack of a sense of humour wasn't one of them. The moment Jonathan stepped on to the village green he felt something terribly wrong. A tingling ran up his body and his hair stood on end as a shrill, keening noise burrowed its way into his head. It took him a moment to realise what it was. Hobbes End was screaming.

Lilith glowed with sickly incandescence as she performed her deadly work. With a final twist of the spear she wrenched reality asunder and opened a gate, not into the realm outside of creation, but to somewhere else entirely. Above her she saw a sheet of black, translucent glass, framing the outline of a pair of mighty wings: Gabriel's wings. The Archdemon stared at the underside of the village pond, the earth fused into ceramic by the force of Gabriel's landing all those years ago. It was here he had given away most of his power to breathe life into Hobbes End, to give it sentience, a soul... a heart. Lilith could feel the love that flowed within the glass; she despised it utterly.

'*To the last, I grapple with thee.*' She screamed. '*From Hell's heart I stab at thee. For hate's sake I spit my last breath at thee, thou damned village!'*

Summoning all the power she could muster, Lilith rammed the spear upward and into the glass. The resulting explosion knocked her to the floor as pond water cascaded downward. Hobbes End shrieked in appalling pain and, as if a candle in the darkness had been snuffed out, the village... died.

Chapter 22

Vladimir

Cay stroked the muzzle of the mother wolf as the cubs rolled and played in the snow at her feet. Mr Peters sat by her side and watched.

'I've always liked wolves,' he said. *'The children of the night, what sweet music they make.'* He chuckled as if he'd told himself a joke.

Cay smiled at him. She'd become quite fond of the old man over the last months, and felt bad about the time she'd spent tormenting him.

A shudder ran through the ground, and the wolves whined and pricked up their ears. Grabbing the cubs they dashed back to their den and hid.

'What was that?' asked Cay.

Mr Peters got to his feet. 'I don't know. Maybe it's...' He didn't have time to finish his sentence before the ground heaved again. Cracking sounds erupted from the forest as trees – their branches heavily laden with snow – came toppling down. An awful scream filled Cay's head and she sank to her knees. Blood ran from her nose and her hands trembled. She looked at Mr Peters and saw that he was slumped against the fallen tree on which they'd been resting. His pale face was now as white as the snow that covered the forest, and he pressed a hand to his forehead as he grunted in pain.

'Something has happened,' he gasped. 'Something terrible.'

'I need to go,' said Cay, shrugging out of her clothes.

Ever the true gentleman, Mr Peters averted his eyes as Cay went through her change.

'Be careful, my little red wolf,' he said to her. 'I will follow as quickly as I can.'

Cay whined and looked in the direction of the village, before turning back to Mr Peters and softly nuzzling his outstretched hand.

'Run, Cay,' he said.

Lifting her head, she howled at the sky and launched herself into the forest. Every sense she possessed told her that something was terribly wrong. The air smelled different, the forest seemed oddly lifeless, as if drained of something profound and magical. Everything felt so... ordinary, and that was terrifying. Snow flew from her paws as she raced along, but with every stride the feeling that she was already too late grew. The world she knew so well was utterly silent around her. Hoping against hope that her friends and family were safe, she dipped her head and ran as if her life depended on it.

Flay watched in stunned admiration as his mistress dragged herself to her feet. Her silk dress was a mess of singed rags and her hands were little more than blackened claws. Even with Michael's Spear, the power needed to destroy the heart of Hobbes End had been unimaginable. Above them the base of the village pond lay sundered, a huge crack running through the imprint of Gabriel's wings. Water trickled down from the spring that fed the pond, but it was cold and lifeless.

Lilith made a horrible croaking sound, and it took Flay a moment to realise that she was laughing. She turned and he caught a glimpse of her true face behind the torn veil. He blanched at the sight of it.

'Go and get the book,' she ordered.

Flay hesitated. He knew the fate that met any evil creature that tried to enter Hobbes End. He was not eager to meet the same fiery death that had taken Rook and Raven. That had become legend, even in Hell.

'Idiot!' snarled Lilith. 'Don't you see what I've done? There *is* no more Hobbes End. I have cut out its very soul. Its death throes will have laid waste to anything in range. There is nothing to stop us now. Go and get the book!'

Flay nodded, checking that his knife was tucked securely in his belt. Climbing onto the edge of the scrying pool, he vaulted upward, clinging to the shattered glass. He half expected his hands to catch fire, but when they didn't he allowed himself a feral grin. He was going to enjoy this.

Shimmying through the gap, Flay found himself standing at the bottom of an unusually deep pond. He turned round and came face to face with the open jaws of the dragon that had vaporised Lilith's giant spider. It took a second for Flay to realise that the dragon was lifeless. Its eyes were dead, and wisps of acrid smoke trickled from gaps in its armoured hide.

'Oh, this is just marvellous,' he said, clambering onto Brass' back and up the muddy bank. The scene of devastation that met his eyes filled him with a sense of immense wellbeing. Smoking fissures spread out from the pond like jagged spokes on a buckled bicycle wheel. To his right, a windmill stood tall against the sky but its wooden sails lay in pieces on the ground. Across the green a row of cottages gaped with empty eyes – their windows cracked and broken – and here and there lay the still bodies of the village inhabitants, silent in the snow.

'Oh, will you look at that,' said Flay. 'Christmas has come early. Who shall I unwrap first?' He toyed with his knife as he pondered whether to gather trophies to add to his hideous armour. 'Perhaps later,' he murmured. 'Once I've got the book. The windmill was the last place we saw it, so there we shall start.'

Taking his time, the harlequin demon strode across the frozen ground, revelling in the fact that there was nobody to stop him. No dragons, no angels, no nothing. He whistled as he walked, his long legs taking him swiftly to his prize. The door to the windmill was open, the bottom hinge torn from the frame and hanging free. Ducking his head inside he was greeted by more temptation than he thought possible. Three men and one cat lay slumped on the floor and, on a nearby table, the book of creation lay on a bed of silk.

'Well, well,' said Flay, giving Lucifer's prone form a derisory prod with the toe of his boot. 'How the mighty have fallen. I wish I could see your face when you awake. See the look in your eyes when you realise how little time you have left, watch you despair as all you helped build is torn apart and fed to the darkness.'

Not seeing any point in further delay, Flay took the book and headed back to the pond. Lost in his smugness, he didn't hear the approaching paws until it was too late. He turned just in time to see the red-furred wolf in mid-air, her jaws open as she struck him head on.

Flay flew backwards and the book slipped from his grasp. He was so surprised, he didn't have time to reach for his knife before Cay sank her fangs into his forearm, thrashing her head and ripping through armour and demon flesh. Flay screamed in pain and fumbled for his knife, slashing out wildly. Cay saw the blow coming and rolled away, grabbing the book in her jaws and speeding off towards the vicarage.

Every sense she had screamed at her to run as fast and as far as she could, but the carnage around her pulled at her heartstrings. The portal to Heaven was gone, and ahead of her she saw Jonathan lying on his side. Behind him, tumbled from their gateposts the gargoyles lay frozen, their little faces pulled taught in agony. She could hear Jonathan breathing, but only just. For a split second she turned her head towards the village shop and her parents, and that was all the opening Flay needed. His knife sang through the frigid air, spinning through flakes of white until it met flesh and bone, catching Cay in her haunches. She howled, dropping the book, but when she tried to run her back legs no longer worked.

She swung to look at her pursuer and whined as Flay strode across the green, his face a mask of grim intent. She'd only managed to crawl two metres when he caught up with her and placed his boot on her neck, forcing her to the ground.

'That's twice you've damaged my armour,' he said, pulling his knife free and making her yelp. 'I need to repair it and some werewolf skin will be a nice addition to my collection. Let me make a delivery and I'll be back for you. Don't run off.'

He whistled as he picked up the book and walked back to the pond. Looking down into the dank, dragon-filled pit, he could see Lilith looking expectantly through the ruin of Gabriel's wings. She smiled wickedly and held out her hands. Flay gave a satisfied nod and carefully dropped the book down to her. She caught it and cradled it to her chest. For the last Archdemon at least, Christmas had indeed come early.

'I won't be a minute,' said Flay. 'I just need to pick up some supplies.' He returned to where Cay was desperately dragging herself towards the forest, a shocking crimson smear behind her on the white snow. She saw him standing over her, knife in hand, and she snarled.

'Now, now, no need for that,' said Flay. 'I must be honest with you, though, this is going to hurt you a lot more than it'll hurt me. So, which bit of your miserable hide will suit me best, hmm?'

He bent down, forced Cay's head to the ground, and raised his knife to begin cutting.

'You... will... not!' said a voice.

Flay turned to see an old man dressed all in black standing behind him. He was breathing heavily as if he'd run himself almost to death.

'And where did you come from?' said Flay. 'You don't look particularly robust. I'm amazed you didn't suffer the same fate as everyone else.'

'Cay and I were at the very edge of the village,' said Mr Peters, 'far enough away not to be rendered helpless.'

'How very handy,' said Flay. 'But if you don't mind I'm going to cut off a piece of her hide. It's kind of my signature thing. I do have a reputation to uphold.'

'I can imagine,' said Mr Peters, 'and I do mind.'

Flay stood up and sighed. 'Look, I really do need to get going and you're beginning to irritate me. I'll kill you if you like but it hardly seems worth it.'

'Ah, I see,' said Mr Peters.

'If you're playing for time you're wasting your breath,' said Flay. 'Nobody here is waking up for quite a while.'

'I know,' said Mr Peters. 'It's just you and me still standing.'

'Life can be so unfair,' said Flay. 'Since you're so polite, I'll make it quick and relatively painless.'

'After what you've done to my friend I will not extend you the same courtesy,' said the old man, taking off his hat and throwing it to the ground. 'I liked the name Vladimir Peters, I have been him for a very long time and he is a good person.' He unbuttoned his long, black coat and let it fall to the ground next to his hat. 'I have had many names over the years. First there was Vlad Tepes, then they called me Vlad Dracul because of my crimes, and then, finally, I became something else. You think you are feared in your patchwork of skin, little demon? Well, I was a nightmare for centuries.'

He turned to Cay where she lay panting on the ground. 'Close your eyes, dear one. Do not see this. Remember me as I was.'

Cay didn't understand what was happening but she did as her friend asked; wondering how Vladimir could stop the demon from killing them both.

'Are you finished?' asked Flay. 'That's it. I'm going to kill you now.'

'No,' said Mr Peters, 'you won't,' and without another word he began to change. Material tore, flesh grew, and a pair of vast membranous wings burst from his back. Bones cracked and reformed, limbs became long and clawed, and his face was no longer anything remotely human.

Even in her wolf form Cay's curiosity could not be held in check, opening her eyes she saw that a monster had taken the place of her friend. A giant, humanoid bat stood in the shredded remains of the old man's clothes. A blunt snout with huge, oval nostrils sat beneath a pair of deep-set crimson eyes, and a horribly long jaw housed razor-sharp teeth with very long canines. He towered over Flay.

'What are you?' gasped Flay, finding himself genuinely surprised.

'The first and now last of my cursed kind,' said Mr Peters, his voice guttural and hoarse. 'In grief I unleashed a plague upon this world, and I spent the rest of my life ending it and seeking forgiveness for what I had done. I am Vladimir, prince of the Carpathian mountains, lord of Wallachia, Moldova and Transylvania, and you, little demon, are mine.'

With a speed that even Flay couldn't match, Mr Peters grabbed him by the wrist and lifted him off his feet. The demon snarled and plunged his knife into Mr Peters' chest, right up to the hilt. It had no effect whatsoever.

Mr Peters grabbed Flay's other arm and held him spreadeagled, his feet kicking at empty air as he dangled above the ground. 'Do you fear me now?' he asked.

Terrified for the first time in his miserable life, Flay could only nod.

'Good,' said Mr Peters. 'It makes you taste better.' Opening his ghastly mouth he sank his teeth into Flay's neck and drank, and drank, until Flay was nothing more than a desiccated husk dressed in a suit of stolen skin. Flinging the body away, Mr Peters looked skyward before sinking to his knees and falling sideways into the snow. He smiled at Cay and she saw no malice in his frightening face, just tears that ran from the corners of his crimson eyes.

'This was my home,' he said to her, his breathing suddenly laboured. 'I could not save it, but with my last act I could at least save you, *meine kleine rote wolfin*. Forgive me, please.'

Whining in pain, Cay dragged herself to Mr Peters' side. He stroked her head gently with his vast, clawed hand. 'I have felt the sun on my face again,' he said, 'and it was good. Goodbye, dear child. Remember me when you run with the wolves.'

Before Cay's eyes Mr Peters' monstrous body crumbled slowly away until there was nothing left but dust. Alone in the ruins of Hobbes End, she raised her head once more and howled her grief at the winter sky.

Chapter 23

Shattered

Jonathan clawed his way to consciousness. His head throbbed and every nerve in his body sang with a dull ache as if suffering the after-effects of electrocution. A sound pierced the fog. It started as a mournful, animal cry, and ended as the uncontrolled sobbing of a girl. Groaning, Jonathan lifted his head and saw Cay kneeling on the green next to a dark patch in the snow. She was wrapped in Mr Peters' coat and crying her heart out.

His strength slowly returning, Jonathan clambered to his feet and staggered over. 'Cay?' he said, kneeling down and wrapping his arms around her.

'He saved me,' she said, once her sobs subsided. 'He knew changing form in the sunlight would kill him but he did it anyway. He was my friend.'

For a moment Jonathan didn't understand, but then the penny dropped as he saw what was left of Flay. 'Mr Peters did that?' he asked.

Cay nodded, reaching out for the fallen hat and clasping

it to her chest. 'I was right after all,' she said. 'He wasn't just a vampire, he was *the* vampire, and he sacrificed himself to save me. I tried to stop Flay from giving the book to Lilith but Flay was too quick. He was going to kill me, but Mr Peters stopped him and now he's just dust.'

Jonathan looked at the black patch on the snow and sighed. 'Oh, Cay, I'm so sorry.'

She wiped her eyes and tried to smile. 'Vlad Dracul, that's what he said he used to be called when he was a prince. He didn't seem to be afraid of dying. He said that he'd felt the sun on his face once again. He said I was his little wolf.' She began sobbing again, softly this time, and Jonathan couldn't think of anything to say to comfort her.

He looked about him and the scale of the devastation became horribly apparent. 'Did you say Flay gave the book to Lilith?' he asked.

Cay nodded. 'He threw it into the pond. I think Lilith did something awful to the village, how else could Flay even be here?'

'How was it you and Mr Peters didn't get affected too?'

'We were with the wolves when it happened, right at the edge of the forest. I think we were far enough away not to get hurt by it.'

'Stay here,' said Jonathan. 'I need to see this for myself.' He got up, and with a sick feeling in his stomach walked over to the pond. With each step the sense of foreboding grew until he was looking down on something he didn't believe possible. The pond was empty of water; the trickle from the spring that filled it ran into a vast crack in the glass base, soaking into the earth beneath. The outline of Gabriel's wings was still there, but the heart of Hobbes End had been cut out. Jonathan desperately reached for some vestige of his grandfather's power, tried to speak to the village that had become his home, but where there had once been a song of joy, where there had once been a soul, there was nothing but a yawning emptiness. 'Oh my God,' said Jonathan, tears streaming down his face.

He felt a touch on his shoulder, and turned to see Ignatius. The vicar looked ashen and his hands were shaking. Jonathan knew how bereft Ignatius must be because he felt the same way.

'What has Lilith done?' said Ignatius. 'How did this happen?'

'She used the spear,' said Jonathan. 'Nothing else is powerful enough to do this. She must have opened up a gate beneath the pond and stabbed the village in its heart, that's what hit us all. It was the sound of Hobbes End dying.'

Ignatius looked about him in a state of shock. 'We need to check if everyone's all right,' he said, desperately trying to get a grip on himself.

'I think everyone will be,' said Jonathan, 'except for Mr

Peters. He... saved Cay's life and killed Flay but...' he looked over to where his friend sat wrapped in the long black coat.

'Oh, Vladimir,' said Ignatius.

'And I think Brass is dead too,' said Jonathan, looking at the dragon as she lay curled at the bottom of the pond, her mouth open and her eyes staring sightlessly upward.

'Monty? Stubbs?' Ignatius gasped, looking over to the vicarage. The twin bodies of the gargoyles lying slumped and rigid in the snow told him his fears had been realised. 'Oh no, no, no,' cried the vicar, looking as though he would weep himself.

Voices began to call out from all around as the villagers woke up from their enforced slumber. 'I need to help them,' said Ignatius.

'It gets worse,' said Jonathan. 'Flay managed to steal the book and give it to Lilith. If I can't stop her then the whole world will die, Ignatius.'

The vicar looked at him and a familiar steely glint came back into his eyes. 'Then you will follow your destiny, my boy,' he said. 'You will leave Hobbes End in my care while you stop that monster. You will not worry about what is happening here, you will not let it distract you. You will fight, not just for us, but for everyone and everything. It's time for you to fly, Jonathan.'

He looked at Ignatius and knew the vicar was right. There was no time to grieve if he was to stop Lilith. There was a final reckoning to be had with the last Archdemon. She would not only pay, but pay dearly.

To Jonathan the next hour passed in a blur. Along with Ignatius he checked on his mother, Cay, Elgar, Sammael, Michael, Constance and everyone else. Cay, in particular, was a matter of great concern. Her father rushed to find her the second he regained consciousness, and discovered the awful wound in her thigh. It was all Jonathan could do to stop Kenneth from turning into a wolf himself and ripping what was left of Flay to pieces. In the end, he agreed to cart off Flay's corpse and make a bonfire with it in his back garden. The act seemed to give Cay's father great satisfaction.

With Flay disposed of, Jonathan helped Grimm carry the gargoyles into Ignatius' study, placing them together in an armchair. The tortured looks on their little faces were almost too much to bear.

'I have no words for this atrocity,' said Grimm, his massive frame shaking with suppressed fury. 'I keep expecting them to say something, like they're just pretending. I...' The big man shook his head. 'This is just too much. How are we going to stop her, Jonathan? This is beyond Ignatius and me. No cricket bats or swords are going to stop Lilith. I don't like feeling so vulnerable.'

'Lucifer will know,' said Jonathan. 'He's pacing round and round the windmill; he's got that look that means he's thinking. I just hope he doesn't take too long about it. Whatever I do I'm going to need his help. We'll need to fight Lilith together or not at all.'

'Yes,' said Grimm. 'Right, I need to go and do the rounds, see what structural damage I have to sort out. Repairs to the village are going to keep me busy for weeks, assuming the world doesn't end.' He stomped out of the vicarage, his shoulders slumped.

'This is really, really bad, isn't it?' said Elgar.

Jonathan nodded. 'I'm gonna fix this, Cat,' he said. 'Lilith has hurt my family, so I'm going to rip Michael's Spear out of her cold, dead hands. Come on, let's go and see Lucifer. I need to know what he wants to do.'

With Elgar at his heels Jonathan made his way to the windmill. He deliberately avoided looking at the pond; the emptiness he felt emanating from it was too awful. He found Lucifer standing in front of the stove, hands clasped behind his back.

'Good, you're here,' he said. 'I was just about to come looking for you.'

'What's the plan?' asked Jonathan.

'Simple,' said Lucifer. 'You and I are going to walk straight into Lilith's palace, kill everything that gets in our way and prise Michael's Spear out of...'

'Her cold dead hands?' said Elgar. 'Yep, already ahead of you on that one.'

'Um?' said Jonathan.

'What?' said Lucifer.

'I was kinda expecting something a bit more... subtle?'

'We're facing the end of the universe,' said Lucifer. 'Subtlety is not what's called for at this point. It's time for some good, old-fashioned brute force. Any questions?'

'So it's just you and me then?'

Lucifer nodded. 'Sam isn't going to be able to do anything but groan in pain for days, and Michael – incredibly strong though he is – is still recovering from being almost dead for centuries. Saving creation is down to the two of us. You up for it?'

Jonathan didn't need to think twice. 'Hell, yeah,' he said.

'Good lad. Hurting Hobbes End will have been a huge drain on Lilith's power. She won't be able to carry out her miserable little plan immediately, but she will recover. We have maybe a day at most before everything comes apart. Say your goodbyes, Jonathan. We come back from this successful or we die in the attempt. You understand?'

'Yeah,' said Jonathan. 'I do.'

'Right, meet me on the green in one hour and don't forget your toothbrush.' With a grim smile fixed firmly on his face, Lucifer strode out of the windmill.

'Blimey, so this is really it then,' said Elgar. 'I guess asking if I could tag along is kinda pointless?'

'Sorry, Cat,' said Jonathan. 'I think things are going to

get messy and I need to know you'll be safe here with everyone else.'

'Oh, thank god for that,' said Elgar. 'For a second I thought you were going to say I should come with you. I'm quite happy waiting for the end of days by curling up in my basket in the kitchen and kissing my bum goodbye.'

Jonathan picked the cat up and gave him a hug. 'Love you, fleabag,' he said.

'Love you too,' said Elgar. 'Please don't get killed, it would be very irritating.'

Jonathan chuckled and put the cat on a chair. 'Right, before I go I need to speak to Sam, and then Mum. See you on the green.'

'Wouldn't miss it,' said the cat as he watched his friend climb the stairs. 'Kick Lilith's butt, Jonny, and don't hold back.'

Jonathan entered the angel's room and found her lying in bed, Michael by her side. 'Did Lucifer tell you what we're going to do?' he asked.

'Yes,' said Sammael, motioning for him to sit on the bed where she could hold his hand. 'You just promise me one thing.'

'What?'

'That you use everything you have in that arsenal of tricks Gabriel left you to destroy Lilith. I heard what Elgar said, don't you dare hold back. Don't be afraid of all that power you have, just open up and give it everything. Be what your grandfather wanted you to be.'

'And what's that?' asked Jonathan.

'True to yourself and your heritage. It *is* time for you to fly, Jonathan. Here we are facing the end of everything and it's just you and Lucifer against the darkness. You couldn't make it up, could you?'

'No,' said Jonathan. 'Life is so strange sometimes. If we survive I may write a book about it. It would be a good story.'

'That it would,' said Sammael.

'I want to come with you,' said Michael, 'but I'd only slow you down. This is my kind of job and here I am a damn invalid.'

'Well, you were technically dead for quite some time,' said Jonathan.

'Pfft! Never let death get in the way of a good fight, that's my motto,' said Michael. 'Fight well, little soldier, and if you get the chance, grab my spear out of her...'

'Cold, dead hands?' suggested Jonathan.

'Exactly,' said Michael, giving him a fierce grin.

'I guess I should go now,' said Jonathan. 'I'll see you both soon.'

'I know you will,' said Sammael, clasping Jonathan's hand and pressing it to her cheek. 'Be brave, my boy.'

He nodded, got up, and left the room without looking back.

Savantha stood in the vicarage kitchen, her arms wrapped tightly around Jonathan. She was trying and failing not to cry. 'My son,' she said, wiping her face. 'It always seems to be you saving someone or something, doesn't it?'

He hugged her back. 'Yeah,' he said, his face buried into her shoulder. 'We'll stop her, Mum. I promise.'

'I know you will, sweetheart. Come back to me, won't you?'

Jonathan nodded. 'Yeah, Mum,' he said. 'I don't want to miss Christmas.'

She took his hand. 'Are you ready?'

'Yeah, I am.'

'Then let's go and finish this once and for all,' she said.

They walked out of the vicarage to find the whole village gathered on the green. Lucifer stood to one side, his face impassive. Jonathan couldn't help but smile as everyone nodded at him and wished him well. They all knew what he was about to risk, not just for them, but for everyone, everywhere.

'This is for you,' said Mrs Flynn, pressing a sherbet lemon into Jonathan's hand. 'For luck.' Jonathan put it in his mouth, the sugary goodness going some way to stop the empty feeling in his stomach.

'Thanks, Mrs F,' he said. 'I'll see you all soon.'

Kenneth Forrester appeared with Cay cradled gently in his huge arms. 'She insisted that there was no way you were going without her waving you off,' he said.

Cay reached out and put her arms round Jonathan's neck before kissing him on the cheek. 'Be stupid,' she said. 'Be magnificent.'

'I'll try.'

'We need to go,' said Lucifer.

Jonathan nodded and went to stand beside him. He looked at all the familiar faces that he'd come to love, and for a moment the weight of what he was about to attempt seemed overwhelming. It was Ignatius who lifted his spirits.

'Remember,' said the vicar. 'There's no point getting old...'

'If you don't get crafty,' replied Jonathan. He turned to Lucifer. 'I'm ready,' he said.

The fallen angel took a deep breath and, as carefully as he could, opened a gate to Hell.

Chapter 24

Inferno

'Where are we?' asked Jonathan as the gate closed behind them.

'Somewhere near Lilith's palace,' said Lucifer. 'Not too near though. She'll be expecting us and I don't want to make this easy for her.'

Jonathan looked around. They were standing at the edge of a vast forest, filled with alien-looking trees draped with wisps of silk thread. 'That's spider web, isn't it?'

'Yep,' said Lucifer. 'We need to be on our toes here. We can't afford to get bitten again. If we do it's game over, as I believe the youth of today would say.'

Jonathan shuddered. He wasn't scared of spiders but he didn't relish the thought of having more venom running through his veins. He'd barely recovered from the last lot.

'Where's Lilith's palace?'

'Somewhere in the middle,' said Lucifer. 'I've never actually seen it but I'm looking forward to razing it to the ground. Come on, let's go.'

They began their walk, and slowly the red sun of Hell was obscured by the canopy of leaves overhead. The forest was utterly silent except for the occasional buzz of some grotesquely large insect. Jonathan watched as one particularly impressive specimen – all dangling legs and long, pointed proboscis – landed on the brightly coloured pad of a huge fern. It was immediately squished as the fern snapped shut like a massive Venus fly trap. The buzzing of the insect grew to a loud squeal as it was rapidly digested, green ooze leaking from toothed gaps in the fern's leaves.

'Ick,' said Jonathan.

'Nature red in tooth and claw,' said Lucifer, brushing strands of web from his face.

'Shouldn't we try and find a path?' suggested Jonathan.

Lucifer shook his head. 'Lilith will have any paths watched and trapped. I want to be as close as we can be before the alarm is raised.' He took a step forward and a spider the size of Jonathan's fist scuttled from the undergrowth, aiming for Lucifer's leg. Without thinking Jonathan summoned his wings and cut the horrible thing in half. It gave a little squeal and deflated as its insides leaked on to the forest floor.

'You're getting better at that,' said Lucifer.

They walked onward, but the silk strung between the trees grew more and more dense until it slowed their progress to a crawl.

'This is taking too long,' said Lucifer, scowling.

Tearing his way through a solid wall of webbing, Jonathan found what appeared to be a trail; the ground was full of small indentations.

'This looks well used,' he said.

'By something with lots of legs,' added Lucifer. 'Still, as it's heading in the right direction we might as well use it for now. Stay sharp.'

Jonathan nodded and, keeping his wings at the ready, he followed the fallen angel. The insect buzzing died away until the forest was utterly silent, the webbing on either side of the trail so thick they couldn't see through it. They hadn't gone far when they emerged into a wide clearing with no other exit.

'That's annoying,' said Lucifer. 'I was hoping we'd get further in before we met resistance.'

'What is this place?' asked Jonathan, a prickling sensation running up the back of his neck.

'An arena, I think,' said Lucifer. 'Don't look up by the way.'

Jonathan swallowed hard and did what he was told. The sensation of being watched was overwhelming, and the silk which shrinkwrapped the edges of the clearing vibrated as if being plucked by hundreds of tiny fingers.

'Why mustn't I look up?' he asked.

'Because I don't want you to scream,' said Lucifer.

Jonathan tried not to imagine what was overhead, but it

didn't take much to figure out what might be dangling from silken threads, waiting to fall upon them.

A faint chittering began and Lucifer tensed. 'You cover us from above. I'll deal with the ground attack. Here they come, you can look now.'

Jonathan glanced up, and just as he'd feared there were six huge spiders plummeting towards them, eyes glittering, legs outstretched and fangs dripping with venom. He lashed out with his wings, filling the air with a mass of razor-edged purple ribbons. Unable to stop their fall the spiders were torn apart. Black and green goo showered everywhere as Lucifer launched his own attack, sending fireballs at the arachnids that came at them from all sides.

It was over in seconds but to Jonathan it felt like an eternity. His pulse raced as he waited for the next wave, but nothing came.

'You OK?' asked Lucifer.

'I think so,' said Jonathan. 'Why have they stopped?'

'I don't know,' said Lucifer. 'Perhaps they—'

He didn't get the chance to finish. All around them, the webs between the trees were torn away to reveal a forest alive with movement. For as far as Jonathan could see, every surface seethed with spiders of all shapes and sizes. They were surrounded by an arachnid army.

'Oh dear,' said Lucifer. 'This may be more difficult than I thought.'

The clearing grew smaller as the spiders crept forward, their myriad legs pitter-pattering on the dead leaves that carpeted the ground.

'We could try flying?' said Jonathan.

Lucifer shook his head. 'The trees are full of them. If only one of them gets a bite in we've had it. Keep very close to me, Jonathan. I don't want you getting hurt.'

'What are you going to do?'

Lucifer was about to answer when the sea of eyes, legs and fangs surged forward. He struck the ground with his fist and a wall of fire sprang up around them, ripping into the trees and toasting anything that came near. An awful crackling began as the forest burst into flame, forcing the spiders back. Sweat beaded on Lucifer's forehead as he collected his will. 'Keep your head down,' he said. 'Things are about to get very, very hot.'

Crouching next to the fallen angel, Jonathan could only stare in amazement as the fire ripped outward with astonishing speed, incinerating everything it touched. The spiders turned to run, but their sheer numbers hampered their escape and they died in their millions, shrieking and chittering as they burned. A circle of blackened destruction blossomed around Jonathan and Lucifer as the roaring inferno consumed the forest. Choking black smoke seared the back of Jonathan's throat as Lilith's terrible army was routed. No matter how fast they ran the flames were faster;

death came for them all. Once he was sure the threat had been eliminated, a soot-smeared Lucifer struggled to his feet.

'Are you OK?' asked Jonathan.

'Yes, just a bit tired, that's all.'

'Why would Lilith sacrifice her entire army if she knew you could do something like that?' Jonathan asked.

'She's wearing us down,' said Lucifer. 'There's only so much power you can wield without taking time to recover. She wants to make sure we're as weak as possible when we face her, and that little trick took some doing I can tell you. Damn spiders.'

'You OK to walk?' asked Jonathan.

'Oh yes,' said Lucifer. 'I don't care what it takes. She knows we're coming but I *will* see Lilith burn. Let's go.'

Surrounded by smouldering wreckage, Jonathan and Lucifer made their way towards the distant remains of the forest. More than once the fallen angel stumbled and Jonathan had to steady him. He wondered how much power it had taken to destroy Lilith's army, and how much Lucifer had left. Neither of them had fully recovered from the spider venom, and now they had to face the last Archdemon in her lair. She'd be waiting for them, and she had Michael's Spear to wield. Jonathan had no idea if the two of them would be enough, but they had no choice in the matter. They would stop her or die trying.

They trudged wearily onward through the acres of flash-fried arachnids that littered their path. The destruction was necessary, but it made Jonathan sad. The spiders were mindless, driven by Lilith's will to serve her. They hadn't deserved such an awful fate. The centre of the forest drew closer, and through trees that still burned Jonathan saw a sprawling wooden structure surrounded by a still, dark lake.

'Is that Lilith's palace?' he asked.

'Yes,' said Lucifer. 'Welcome to the belly of the beast.'

'Should we try and sneak in?' said Jonathan.

Lucifer shook his head. 'She knows we're here, subtlety is pointless. We march right up to her front door and kick it in. All her focus will be on preparing to destroy creation. It's a race, Jonathan. A race to see which of us has the strength to do what needs to be done. Are you ready for that?'

The look in Lucifer's eyes made Jonathan shrink back. This was the first Morningstar, the angel that had read the universe into being. The implacable will behind that sternly-handsome face was something Jonathan could barely comprehend. It scared him.

'I asked if you were ready?' said Lucifer, seeing the conflict inside Jonathan.

'I think so.'

Lucifer's gaze softened. 'You will do your best. You are Gabriel's grandson, remember that. He'd be proud of you.

Sometimes all the choices you have left are difficult ones, and when that happens you have to choose the one that hurts the least. Gabriel knew that to be true, do you?'

Jonathan nodded. They had no choice but to kill Lilith by whatever means necessary. If they didn't she would rip their universe apart and laugh while she did it.

'I understand,' he said. 'I'm ready.'

Lucifer smiled, genuine warmth in his face. 'I quite like that it's just us two, right here, right now, trying to stop the end of all things. It feels oddly right, somehow.'

Jonathan smiled back. It did feel oddly right. 'Let's go get her,' he said.

'That's my boy,' said Lucifer.

Marching through the last of the forest, they reached the end of the wooden bridge that spanned the lake. 'Be ready for anything,' said Lucifer as he stepped forward. Jonathan followed him, keeping his wings at the ready. Ahead of them, a pair of double doors stood open.

'Does this feel a bit too easy?' asked Jonathan.

'I don't know,' said Lucifer. 'She may have kept some spiders in reserve so watch your feet. We can't afford to get bitten when we're so close.'

Fully expecting to be attacked from every direction, Jonathan followed Lucifer into Lilith's palace. It was beautiful in its own way, carved from closely-grained wood and fitted together by the hands of a craftsman. It felt wrong that such amazing construction should be used to house such a monster.

They emerged into a huge inner courtyard with a small grove of silk-wrapped trees at its centre.

'That's where she'll be,' said Lucifer, 'right at the heart of her realm. Don't hold back, Jonathan. If she gives you an opening, use those wings of yours to tear her apart. Use everything that Gabriel gave you.'

Jonathan nodded, but his mouth was dry and his chest tight. Fear was a difficult thing to control, and knowing that Lilith had a spear that could kill him with the slightest touch filled him with dread.

They arrived at the entrance to the grove and followed the well-trodden path that led between the ghostly trees, everything still and silent as they spiralled towards the centre. They couldn't be more than a few steps from Lilith and Jonathan's hands shook.

'Here we are,' whispered Lucifer as they reached the final turn. 'Whatever she's doing give her everything you've got. On three: one... two... three!'

They stepped out, ready to attack, only to be faced by the sight of an empty clearing with a pool of water at its heart.

'I don't understand,' said Lucifer. 'Where is she? This is the centre of her realm, the seat of her power; she needs to be here to carry out her plan. She wouldn't be strong enough anywhere else.'

Jonathan was only half listening to Lucifer. The second he saw the empty clearing he knew they'd been tricked. Gabriel's insight was part of him now, and his mind was already working on where the Archdemon had gone. If she'd left the seat of her power she must be somewhere that would help her achieve her goal, somewhere that was already damaged enough to make it easy for her to tear creation apart.

The answer was so obvious it hit Jonathan like a sledgehammer. 'I know where she is,' he said to Lucifer, 'and I think we may be too late.'

Chapter 25

My Gift to You

'I can't just sit here!' growled Michael.

'What else can you do?' asked Sammael as she lay in bed, her face pale.

'I'm a warrior, dammit. I won't let them go up against Lilith alone.'

'But you're nowhere near up to strength yet. How would you open a gate to wherever they are?'

Michael gave her a smile filled with such warmth that she had to hold back tears. '*I* can't open a gate, but maybe someone else will do it for me?'

'I don't understand?' said Sammael.

'You will, dear sister. Remember that I love you.' He kissed her on the forehead and ran downstairs.

'What are you doing, Michael?' Sammael cried out, but he was gone. If she'd been able to move she would have followed him, but the pain of trying to sit up was too great. All she could do was lay back and hope her little brother didn't do something irredeemably stupid.

Michael left the windmill and crossed the green to the pond. He half climbed, half slid down the bank until he was standing on the shattered outline of Gabriel's wings. The vast bulk of Brass' lifeless body was a stark reminder of what they had lost, of what Gabriel had achieved during his long life.

'You showed us all what wonderful things a willing sacrifice can create, my brother,' Michael whispered. 'I may not be an engineer, but there is one thing I do have that may be of use. I have a mighty heart, and I'm going to share it with you.'

Taking a deep breath, Michael knelt on the glass and willed his wings to appear; nothing happened. His brow furrowed in concentration as he summoned every ounce of his strength, dug into all the sunlight that Sammael and Jonathan had used to bring him back from the brink of death. At first they began as pale shadows, but Michael had never run from a fight in his life. He gave everything he had, and his wings answered him.

From his shoulders, a cluster of ribbons unfurled to meet the sky. White as the snow that covered the village, pure and new, they sang their song of joy. Michael allowed himself one perfect moment, revelling in their power, their beauty, and in the next breath he gave them away.

Plunging the ribbons downward he called out to Gabriel's legacy, called out to Hobbes End, and just like his brother before him freely let slip the most precious gift he could offer. His wings slid into the damaged glass, melded with it and faded from his shoulders. The sense of loss he felt at that moment was impossible to describe. It was as though he'd been split in two. He knew he would never fly again, but he was far from powerless. He still had his mighty heart, and it beat so strongly in his chest that he knew he could bear the pain of such bereavement.

Slumping to the floor of the pond he laid his cheek against the cold glass and called out to his brother. 'Can you hear me, Gabriel?' he asked as snowflakes fell gently upon him. 'It's my gift to you. Please let it be enough.'

For long moments Michael lay in silence, his shoulders and heart aching, wondering if his sacrifice was pointless. He was just about to close his eyes and pray when he received the answer he'd been waiting for.

Thump thump

'I hear you,' said Michael. 'Now come back to us, please.'

Thump thump

Michael climbed stiffly to his feet and watched as the damage beneath him began to mend itself. Slowly at first, but with increasing speed the jagged edges knit together until there was no sign that Lilith had ever been there. The outline of Gabriel's body and wings was still clear, but now streaks of glorious white shot through the black glass: Michael's sacrifice, and his gift. The heart of Hobbes End was whole once more, and it beat as strongly as Michael's own.

He reached out to lay a hand on Brass' head, and smiled as light bloomed in her eye sockets. 'Attagirl,' he said to her. 'Attagirl.'

'Where has she gone?' Lucifer demanded, furious that he'd been tricked.

'The only place she could go if she wasn't here,' said Jonathan.

'Where?'

'Baal's castle. Lilith's gone to where creation was wounded the most, where Sam ripped it open and threw Baal's soul into the darkness. She can cut open the same place with ease.'

Lucifer looked at him in horror. 'We need to get there now,' he gasped. 'Just give me a second.'

Jonathan watched as Lucifer gathered his strength to open a gate one final time. Sweat beaded on the fallen angel's brow as he struggled with obvious exhaustion. Lucifer was possibly the most powerful being in all of creation, but even he had his limits. The spider venom and the constant fighting had taken their toll, and his skin looked grey as he carefully pulled aside the weave to reach their destination.

'In!' Lucifer shouted, and they dived through the gate

which slammed shut behind them, almost too close for comfort.

Jonathan recognised their location immediately; they were in Baal's throne room. Standing nearby was Lilith, spear in one hand and book in the other. Behind her, a rip in the fabric of creation over three metres high bled light and life into infinite darkness. Jonathan knew they were too late; the incision Lilith had made was mortal. She'd used the corrupted power of Michael's Spear, and there was nothing they could do to stop the wound from growing until it swallowed everything.

'How nice of you to join me,' the Archdemon said. 'I wanted you to see this so you'd know just how total your failure was. Enjoy your deaths, they should be quite unpleasant.'

Lilith turned to enter the rip, but Lucifer launched a fireball that scorched the air as it flew. The Archdemon fended it off with ease.

'Tired, are we?' she mocked. 'Goodbye, *old friend.*'

Jonathan didn't realise what he was doing until he was airborne. His wings – outstretched and glorious – sent him hurtling towards Lilith with the speed and grace of a falcon. The equations for flight resolved themselves in his head, a beautiful simplicity that defied gravity. For the first time in his life, Jonathan slipped the surly bonds of earth completely under his own control, and it was magnificent.

He struck Lilith at full speed, his wings arched protectively around him. The Archdemon slammed into the wall and the book spun from her hands. With a screech she dived for it, only to be met by Lucifer who grabbed her wrists and tried desperately to wrest the spear from her grasp.

'What have you done!' he bellowed.

'Destroyed your work,' she spat back. 'The end is coming and there's nothing you can do to stop it.'

An awful tearing sound came from behind Jonathan as the rip lengthened. The weave had been severed, and all of creation would unravel if he didn't do something. Still airborne, he rushed to the centre of the rip, using his wing ribbons to grasp the tattered edges of reality as tightly as he could. He knew he couldn't heal the wound; the damage was too great, all he could do was hold creation together with every ounce of strength he had. Suspended like a fly in a spider's web, he screamed in pain as every convulsion in the weave threatened to tear him apart.

'See!' shrieked Lilith. 'Even Gabriel's grandson can't stop it. We can fight here until he dies if you like? The result will be the same. You are old, Lucifer, a shadow of your former self, weak and soft. Your time is over, and mine is come!'

With shocking strength, Lilith rammed the spear haft into Lucifer's stomach and sent him sprawling. She turned to Jonathan where he hung helpless, trying to save not only his home, but the entire universe.

'See me, boy,' said Lilith. 'See me as I truly am.' With a series of awful cracking noises her lower body morphed. Just like Belial before her she liked to keep her true self hidden, but now she wanted Jonathan to witness the horror he was up against before he died.

Her silk dress shredded as a vast, bloated spider's abdomen, complete with eight multi-jointed legs, burst into view. Her torso remained that of a woman, rearing upright and with Michael's Spear still in her hands. For a horrible finale she ripped away her veil to reveal a face that was almost human, except for the eight black orbs that dotted her forehead.

'Behold, child,' she cried in triumph. 'See the queen of the silk garden and know that she has undone you all!' Cackling with glee, Lilith drew back her arm and threw the spear directly at Jonathan's chest. 'Die!' she screamed.

Time slowed to a crawl as Jonathan watched the deadly tip of the spear arc towards him. He felt strangely calm, knowing that death was inevitable but refusing to let slip the tattered edges of creation. If he was going to die he would do it with honour, fighting to the last just as Gabriel had done. He closed his eyes and waited for the pain, but none came.

Lilith shrieked in rage, and opening his eyes once more Jonathan saw Lucifer standing in front of him, their faces barely a metre apart. The tip of Michael's Spear protruded from the fallen angel's chest, and around it, a crimson flower blossomed.

Jonathan opened his mouth to speak but no words came. He looked at Lucifer and saw no fear, only pride, not in himself, but at the fact Jonathan hadn't let go with his wings when he'd seen death coming for him.

'I'm so sorry,' said Lucifer, before falling to a crumpled heap on the floor.

. Fetching the book from where it lay, Lilith scuttled over on those horrible legs, fixing her black, multi-eyed gaze on the helpless Jonathan. 'Time to end this,' she said with an evil grin.

Chapter 26

A Stitch in Time

Jonathan hung in the air, pinned to the rip in creation with the tips of his toes far above the ground. The only thing stopping the destruction of everything was the strength of his wings and his belief in himself. Air rushed past him into the awful void at his back; he could feel the cold emptiness gnawing at him like a rabid dog. At his feet, Lucifer groaned as his life blood pooled on the floor of Baal's throne room.

'I think I'll wait and watch you die,' said Lilith, pulling the spear free of Lucifer's body. 'It's ironic that the thing you are trying to save will be the thing that kills you, don't you think?'

Jonathan could only grunt in pain as another shudder ran through creation. Despite his best efforts the rip lengthened just a little more.

'Not much longer,' said Lilith.

Jonathan looked up, and to her irritation he gave the Archdemon a smile, despite the agony he endured. Worse still, he began humming a tune to himself.

'I'm glad you find this so amusing,' said Lilith. 'It will make your end all the more unbearable.'

Jonathan shook his head. He hadn't believed it at first, but on the far side of the throne room a miracle was unfolding. Behind it was a song so sweet that it filled his heart. It was Hobbes End, and it was singing 'Amazing Grace'. Jonathan found himself laughing until tears ran down his cheeks. At that moment he felt as though he could do anything.

'Look behind you,' he said to Lilith.

'Oh, child, do you think me such a fool?' she replied.

'No, really,' said Jonathan. 'Look behind you.'

Despite herself Lilith turned, and was rooted to the spot by what she saw. A huge portal had opened in the air, its edges woven with beautiful formulae, celestial mechanics beyond comprehension. Through it strode Michael, clad in a suit of fearsome black-glass armour. Behind him, arrayed across the portal was the entire population of Hobbes End. They were all looking at Lilith, and their faces showed not a trace of fear, only anger and disgust.

Ignatius stood between Savantha and Constance, Grimm supported the injured Sammael, and Cay lay in her father's arms with her mother at her side. Around them were Professor Morgenstern, Angus McFadden, Clara and Cecily Haywood, Mr and Mrs Flynn, Mrs Silkwood and all the others. And there at the back, towering over them all was

Brass, alive and well with Elgar, Montgomery and Stubbs standing proudly on her head. Jonathan's family was here, and if there was one thing they didn't do it was run from a fight.

'You!' growled Michael as he approached Lilith. 'You have something that belongs to me.'

'It's mine now!' screamed the Archdemon, swinging the spear at Michael in a wide arc. He didn't flinch for a second. With extraordinary reflexes, he snapped up a mailed fist and caught the spear before its blade could touch him. Lilith tried to tear it from his grasp, but it wouldn't budge. Michael's grip was like iron, and under that armour beat something so strong it could shatter mountains.

Watching the scene unfold, Jonathan sensed something new in the song of Hobbes End. It wasn't just his grandfather's power that lay beneath it now, there was something else, something beautiful, something that smelled like petrichor: the scent of the dry and thirsty earth after a spring rain. Michael had given his wings to save Hobbes End's life and now he was part of it, too, just like Gabriel. And in gratitude the village had given everything it could back to the angel, granting him the power to open the portal and defeat the Archdemon once and for all.

Lilith and Michael seemed frozen in time as they played their deadly tug-o-war with the spear. Its runes blazed as Lilith tried to incinerate the angel, but try as she might he stood firm. He was not alone. Hobbes End was with him; Gabriel was with him; and the power they shared was more than a match for the Archdemon's hatred. Michael's armoured fist glowed with heat, but he didn't flinch for a second. He closed his eyes, and asked the weapon that had been forged for him by his siblings to do one thing. *Come home.*

And the spear, disgusted at what it had been forced to do, answered him. Slowly, and to Lilith's dismay, first the blade and then the haft lost their virulence. Rune by rune the crimson energy faded until the spear burned white like sunlight on snow, white like the heart of a star. Lilith shrieked as the weapon turned on her, searing her hand to ashes.

Triumphant, Michael held the spear over his head, basking in its radiance, feeling the warmth on his scarred face. After suffering alone in the dark for so many years, he was once again the warrior angel he had been born to be.

'This, Monster,' he said, 'is mine!' Gripping the haft in both hands, he swung the spear with all his strength, cutting Lilith's horrible legs out from under her with one incredible blow.

She howled and toppled to the floor of the throne room, the book spilling from her one remaining hand.

'I really hate spiders,' said Michael. He brought the spear back for one final strike, but stopped as something occurred to him. 'Grimm,' he said. 'I believe you had something to say to Lilith?'

'Oh, I certainly do,' said Grimm, walking forward until he towered over the writhing Archdemon. At his side he held his favourite cricket bat, Isobel.

'Now then,' said Grimm. 'Your man Flay, who – for your information – made very good kindling, said something while he was trying to kill Cay that I take issue with. He said, and I quote, *this is going to hurt you a lot more than it's going to hurt me.*'

Lilith looked at him with eight, unblinking eyes, and gulped.

Just as he had when he'd fought Crow of the Corvidae, Grimm swung Isobel as hard as he could and took Lilith's vile head clean off her shoulders. It sailed across the throne room, past Jonathan, and disappeared into the void behind him. Jonathan couldn't help but notice that the last expression on Lilith's face was one of surprise.

'Hit for six!' called Elgar.

Leaving the twitching corpse of the Archdemon where she lay, Michael grabbed the book and ran to where Jonathan hung in the air. The wind had stopped rushing through the rip and an ominous silence filled the room.

'What do I do?' asked Michael.

Jonathan was about to answer when Lucifer did it for him. 'You can't do anything,' he said, groaning in pain as he climbed to his feet with Michael's help. Jonathan saw just how much blood was on the floor and his heart sank.

'I'm dying,' said Lucifer. 'There's nothing any of us can do to stop that. I'm going to hold the weave together while Jonathan uses the spear to cauterise the wound. He's the only one strong enough.'

'But how are we going to swap places?' asked Jonathan.

'I'll step outside creation and deal with things from there,' said Lucifer. 'There's no other way.'

'But you'll be trapped,' said Michael, 'with *them*!' The angel glanced past Jonathan into the void and blanched visibly. Emerging from the darkness was an armada of monsters, a seething mass of old and vicious gods that wanted nothing more than to devour them.

'My life is almost done, Michael,' said Lucifer. 'Give me the book and let me do this. My death may save the universe I helped create. It is fitting.'

'There must be another way,' said Michael.

Lucifer shook his head, pressing a hand to his chest in a vain attempt to slow the bleeding.

'Please,' begged Jonathan. 'Just do as he says. We have so little time left.'

Michael looked at his old foe. There was something in Lucifer's eyes that he'd never seen before. He pressed the book into the fallen angel's hands. 'With my blessing,' he said.

'You do have a mighty heart, Michael,' said Lucifer,

tucking the book inside his jacket. 'Watch over them all for me, especially Elgar, I'm rather fond of him.'

Michael nodded.

'Jonathan,' said Lucifer. 'I wish we had more time. There are so many stories to tell. I just wanted you to know that I'm... proud of you.'

Jonathan smiled at him, knowing just how big that compliment was.

'When I say so, let go of the rip. I'll be taking the strain so don't think about anything but mending the weave. I'll only be able to bring the edges together for a few seconds so you must be ready. Do you understand?'

Jonathan nodded, but his face couldn't hide the fear that ran through him. If he failed they would lose *everything*.

'Just remember who and what you are,' said Lucifer. 'All you need to do is believe in yourself, my boy. Don't be afraid.' The fallen angel gave one last look over his shoulder at the assembled crowd in the portal, and slipped past Jonathan's legs and into darkness. Floating in nothing and with an alien army racing towards him, Lucifer spread his wings and summoned everything he was into one last effort. Grasping at the tattered edges of reality, he sank his very being into the threads and pulled.

'NOW, JONATHAN!' he shouted.

With a cry of relief Jonathan dropped to the floor. He reached out to take the spear from Michael, but just before his hand closed upon it he hesitated. What if the spear rejected him? It had been tortured for centuries by Lilith, how would it react to being used by someone who was half demon? What if it thought he wasn't worthy?

Michael saw the torment in Jonathan's eyes. 'Labels, names, titles, they mean nothing,' he said. 'All that matters is what is in your heart, and yours is as mighty as mine. Here, take it, she will not fail you.'

Shaking, Jonathan's fingers closed around the haft of the spear; the power that lay within it was vast. In Gabriel's memories, Jonathan could see and feel the hammer strokes that had forged the weapon. It had been created to destroy, but now it was being used to heal.

'Will you help me?' Jonathan asked. 'Will you help someone who is half-angel, half-demon?' From deep inside the spear Jonathan heard what sounded like laughter, as if the question he had just asked was a silly one.

'Yes,' the spear whispered to him.

Shuddering with relief Jonathan turned to Lucifer. The fallen angel was in obvious agony as he held the universe together, but he looked Jonathan in the eye and gave him a triumphant smile.

'Told you,' said Lucifer, gathering his remaining strength. 'On the count of three, my boy.'

Jonathan nodded and raised the spear.

'One.'

Jonathan sank his will into the weapon, feeling the energy build.

'Two.'

He felt a hand on each of his shoulders as both Michael and Sammael came to stand with him, offering their support and adding their power to his. They were a family, and they would face this together.

'THREE!' His face contorted with effort, Lucifer slammed reality shut.

Without conscious thought Jonathan opened himself to the spear. The blade flared an incandescent white, and a blast of purest energy struck the wound that threatened to tear the universe apart. Jonathan saw the threads of the weave melt and reform, bathed in a loving sea of molten mathematics. He gave everything he had, and any doubts about what he might be capable of were burned away. Jonathan finally knew who he was, and it was wonderful.

Unable to contain so much power, the spear shattered in his hands, filling the air with a glittering cloud and sending Jonathan, Michael and Sammael sprawling. Silence filled the throne room, and through watering eyes Jonathan looked to where the rip had been. It was gone, with no sign in the weave that there had ever been any damage.

Both deep inside him and impossibly far away, Jonathan felt rather than heard a single word of farewell.

'Goodbye,' said Lucifer.

'Goodbye,' Jonathan replied, and, cradled against Michael's broad chest, he wept.

Hanging in the void outside of reality, Lucifer sighed with relief. The universe he had read into being was safe once more, and in the hands of a worthy successor. On all sides, a vast array of tentacles and teeth drew close but the fallen angel ignored them. His vision dimming as death approached, he reached into his jacket and took out the book he'd first held at the beginning of time itself. He stroked the smooth glass with numb fingers and smiled. 'Well, here we are again, old friend,' he said. With his last breath, he read the formula etched onto the page and closed his eyes.

'Let there be light,' he said.

And there was.

Chapter 27

Once More, with Feeling

Hobbes End was finally at peace. At midnight on Christmas Eve everyone crowded into the church and sang their hearts out. Savantha held Jonathan's hand, but she could see his thoughts were elsewhere. They had lost much over this last year; hopefully Lucifer's sacrifice would be the last one that was ever needed.

Christmas morning came, but rather than open his presents Jonathan asked if he could go and see Cay.

'Of course you can, darling,' said Savantha, kissing him on the cheek.

Wisps of cloud drifted across a clear winter sky as Cay unpacked her new kite in the centre of the green.

'So you're finally going to show me how to fly this thing?' asked Jonathan as he walked up.

'Yep,' said Cay. 'There's not much wind though. I wish we were higher, and the top of the church tower is still off limits.'

Jonathan smiled at her.

'What?' she said. 'Have I got something in my teeth?' She bared them at Jonathan in a mock snarl.

'No,' he said, shaking his head. 'Just get flying.'

'Fine,' said Cay, grabbing hold of the control handles. 'Stand back and watch in awe.' With a flick of her wrists, the kite, a huge rectangle of blue and purple, rose gently into the air.

'Ah, I wish there was more wind,' she said. 'I can't show you all the funky stuff I can do with this baby without it.' Jonathan stepped close behind her and put his hands round her waist. 'Easy, tiger,' she said, wondering what Jonathan was doing.

'Trust me,' he said in her ear.

'OK,' she said, fixing her gaze upward. Safe in Jonathan's arms she flew her kite, flicking it this way and that with small, neat, tugs of the controls. The wind picked up and with the increased pull she unleashed ever more complex tricks, the kite a blur of colour as it flashed across the sky.

Jonathan could feel Cay's chest as it heaved with little sobs.

'What's wrong?' he asked her.

She wiped her eyes on her sleeve and leaned back. 'You've done it, haven't you?' she said, smiling through her tears. 'You've figured it out. Dare I look down?'

'Only if you promise not to scream,' said Jonathan, holding her even more tightly.

Cay nodded, and parking the kite high above her, she looked down at the green some twenty metres below. Supporting her feet was a platform of serrated purple ribbons. She looked over her shoulder, and rippling in the air behind her Jonathan's magnificent wings drank in the winter sun. He'd unfurled them so gently, and lifted her with such care that she hadn't even noticed.

'I have no words,' she gasped.

'You don't need any,' he said. 'I'll never let you fall.'

'I know,' she said, and taking control of her kite once more she launched into a series of extraordinary acrobatics, revelling in the feeling of being so high, and yet so safe.

'For I have slipped the surly bonds of earth,' she whispered.

'And danced the skies, on laughter-silvered wings,' Jonathan whispered back.

And so the two friends hung there, far above the village they called home: a place of safety, of hope, and of family.

'That really is something isn't it?' said Grimm, leaning on one of the vicarage gateposts.

'Yep,' said the gargoyles in unison.

'Well done, great-nephew,' said Sammael, walking arm in arm with Michael to stand by Grimm. 'Looks like he's finally got the hang of it.'

'Well, this is a day of surprises,' said Ignatius as he joined them. 'It's quite handy they're out of the way, actually. It'll give us a chance to get ready.'

'Indeed,' said Grimm. 'Our guests will be here soon.'

'Better go and put the kettle on,' said Ignatius.

'Ah, tea, the solution to all of life's problems,' chuckled Grimm as he turned and walked back down the drive.

It was a good twenty minutes before Cay got tired and Jonathan lowered them both to the ground. The snow crunched beneath their feet as they carefully packed away the kite.

'Where's Elgar?' asked Cay. 'I thought he'd have been out here gawking and pretending not to be impressed.'

'Yeah, that is odd,' said Jonathan. 'He's been a bit quiet the last day or so. Come on. Let's go and get a hot drink, I'm chilly.'

They trudged across the green, and when they reached the vicarage gates the gargoyles hopped off their perches.

'Most impressive,' said Montgomery.

'What he said,' agreed Stubbs.

'Thanks, boys,' said Jonathan. 'You coming in too?'

'Yep,' they said.

Together, they walked down the drive and opened the front door, only to find the vicarage full of people drinking mugs of tea and chatting happily.

'Why is everyone here?' asked Cay.

'Good question,' said Ignatius, leaving his study. 'Follow me.'

Cay looked at Jonathan who shrugged his shoulders. They followed the vicar into the packed kitchen to see three figures standing by the back door: a man, a woman and a boy. The adults were unfamiliar, but the boy in the centre waved and smiled at Jonathan.

'Delius?' he gasped. 'What the...?'

The young demon walked over and gave Jonathan a hug. 'Hi,' he said.

Savantha handed Jonathan and Cay a mug of hot chocolate. 'May I introduce Delius' parents. They've come to visit.'

'Call me Bob,' said the man. 'And this is my wife, Emily.'

Jonathan and Cay smiled and shook their hands, then looked around for the one person that was still strangely absent.

'But if Delius and his parents are here, then where's...?' Cay let the sentence go unfinished as the house went silent.

'Just listen,' said Ignatius, a sad smile on his face as he stood next to Constance and gave her hand a squeeze.

'But...'

'Hush now,' said the vicar, blinking away tears that suddenly filled his eyes.

Cay and Jonathan looked at each other, not knowing what to think. They were about to protest when the first, soft notes of piano music filtered through from the drawing room. It was a simple, haunting melody that spoke of village greens, of cricket, of cups of tea, and of peace.

'What is that?' asked Jonathan.

Ignatius wiped the tears from his face as he listened. 'It's my favourite tune,' he said softly. 'One day, not long after I lost Angela and David, I was sitting at the piano and playing it when a visitor arrived. It's called "Nimrod", and it was composed by Edward...'

'Elgar,' gasped Cay, finishing the sentence.

Ignatius nodded and smiled. 'Elgar,' he said.

'But who's playing the piano?' asked Jonathan.

'Go and see, darling,' said Savantha.

He hesitated until Cay gripped his hand. 'C'mon,' she said, and they made their way past smiling villagers and entered the drawing room. It was empty, except for a young boy sitting on the piano stool and playing with such joy that it brought a lump to their throats. He was dressed in jeans and a shirt, and perched on top of a mop of spiky black hair was a pair of round, wire-framed glasses. He finished playing, waited for the final notes to die away, and turned round to face them.

'Opposable thumbs!' he said, giving them both a toothy grin. 'Wonderful invention, makes playing anything more complicated than "Chopsticks" entirely possible.'

Jonathan and Cay stared, their mouths wide open.

The boy kept grinning, his freckled face and green, twinkling eyes looking so familiar and yet completely alien. He got up and walked over to Cay, put his arms around her and pretended to be sick down her back. She shuddered, burst into tears, and hugged him as hard as she could.

'Elgar?' said Jonathan.

'Blimey, will everyone just stop crying!' he said, rolling his eyes. 'Mum, Dad, Delius, Ignatius, Grimm, Mrs Silkwood and her aspidistra, it's turning into a total blubfest.'

'How...?' said Jonathan, hugging them both.

'Lucifer,' said Elgar. 'He wasn't such a bad sort after all. Just before Lilith attacked the village he gave me a Christmas present. It was a copy of *Pinocchio*. He'd even signed it, and underneath he'd written the words to undo Belial's curse. He'd been able to do it all along, cheeky fallen angel. Hey, check this out!'

Elgar returned to the piano stool and, with astonishing speed, the boy disappeared, only to be replaced by a very familiar black cat. 'Gotta love reversible curses,' he said, changing back. 'It even does my clothes so I don't have to get all naked, unlike some.'

'I am so jealous,' said Cay.

Elgar beamed happily.

Everyone crammed into the room. Elgar's parents and brother stood next to the piano, and Grimm, Constance,

Ignatius, Savantha, Sammael and Michael came to stand behind Jonathan and Cay, along with Mr and Mrs Forrester.

'This is for everyone we've loved and lost,' said Elgar. 'It's for Angela and David, for Gabriel, for Darriel, for Raphael, for Mr Peters and for Lucifer.' He interlocked his fingers, cracked his knuckles, and turned to face the keyboard. 'Once more now,' he said, 'with feeling.'

The delicate melody of 'Nimrod' emerged from the piano, drifted across the room, out of the open windows, and into the white and shining world outside.

Epilogue

Paint the Sky with Stars

A naked Lucifer awoke on a hillside covered in lush, green grass and surrounded by a vast forest. He blinked sleep from his eyes and knew instinctively that his slumber had been very long indeed. He gently probed his chest and found that the wound from Michael's Spear had healed; there wasn't even a scar.

Around him a new and completely alien world teemed with life, and on the horizon twin suns dipped slowly behind a range of mountains, bathing the landscape with a warm, golden light. Above him, the night sky was a bowl of darkest blue, painted with stars.

He got slowly to his feet to survey this new world. Unconsciously he flexed his shoulders and was surprised to feel the absence of the huge, bat-like wings he'd worn since his fall. A look of puzzlement crossed his face, closely followed by a smile. He closed his eyes and asked for something he'd not considered he would ever see again.

From his upper back, a fan of golden ribbons sprang into

being, rippling in the air, soaking up the last rays of sunlight. Craning his head to look behind him, Lucifer was surprised to find tears running down his cheeks. 'Well now,' he said, wiping his face with his hand. 'I wasn't expecting that. Right then, let's see what's what.'

Chuckling quietly to himself, the first Morningstar walked down the hillside. As he did so, the words of a Robert Frost poem popped into his head. '*The woods are lovely, dark and deep, but I have promises to keep, and miles to go before I sleep*,' he whispered. Wearing his new wings with pride and eager to find out what adventures awaited him, Lucifer disappeared beneath the canopy of trees.

Author's Note:

'Everything has to come to an end, sometime,' wrote L. Frank Baum in 1904 in his book, *The Marvellous Land of Oz*, and so it is with Hobbes End and its inhabitants. I've been living with them for a long time and it's difficult to let them go, but I hope, dear reader, that you think I've given them a good send off.

The hymn, 'Amazing Grace', which is sung by the villagers, was published in 1779 with words written by clergyman, John Newton. It's quite beautiful and I couldn't think of anything more fitting to describe Michael's resurrection. The poem, 'High Flight', written by John Gillespie Magee Jr in August 1941 also makes another appearance, and has been a running theme throughout the trilogy. For me, the words describe perfectly how an angel might feel about flying.

Lilith quotes from *Moby Dick* when she stabs Hobbes End in the heart with Michael's Spear. The book, by Herman Melville, was published in 1851, and the image of Captain Ahab attacking the great white whale with his harpoon came to mind while I was writing the scene. As far as Lilith is concerned Hobbes End is her Moby Dick, and the hate she has for it is no less than Ahab's for his whale. Just like the obsessed Captain, Lilith's actions lead to her own destruction.

Lucifer's parting words to us are from Robert Frost's poem, 'Stopping by Woods on a Snowy Evening', written in 1922.

Finally, the lovely Mr Peters reveals his true nature to Cay when he sacrifices himself to save her life. When he is watching the wolf cubs with her he jokingly refers to 'the children of the night'. This is a quote from Bram Stoker's novel, *Dracula*, published in 1897, and is a hint to his true nature. Cay was right about him all along, but just like everyone who comes to Hobbes End a second chance is offered if they are willing to take it with both hands.

And so it is time finally to say goodbye, to all the ones we have loved and lost. Will there be other adventures for Jonathan, Cay, Elgar and the gargoyles? Well that, as they say, is another story.